S&B RA

PRESENTS

A CINCO PESO PRODUCTION

TO KILL A HORSE

BY WILLIAM J. CHAMBERS MSed.

First edition

**Executive Production Manager
Susan R. Hairrell**

**Edited by
Glory Ann Kurtz**

**S&B Ranch Publishing
P.O. Box 1338
Boyd Texas 76023**

**COPYRIGHT BY WILLIAM J. CHAMBERS MSed.
2012 - All Rights Reserved**

No part of this book may be used or reproduced in any manner whatsoever without written permission from the publisher, except in brief quotations within articles or reviews.
For orders and information, contact William Chambers, PO Box 1338, Boyd, Texas 76023

DEDICATION

It doesn't seem like it has been almost three years since the passing of Bob Kurtz, I guess it's because I miss him as much now as I did then. Sometimes I can close my eyes and still see his smile.

I was not the only one touched by this old horse trainer's life or his death. Everyone I have ever talked to who knew Bob was touched in one way or another.

Susan, the lady who introduced me to Bob years ago, is one of those folks. She worked for Bob for many years on his place and is still there, in many ways she's still working for him. They were kindred equine spirits in their love for horses.

As for me, it is hard to find the words. What I can say is, "Bob made me laugh, sometimes he made me mad and when he passed, he made me cry. I still visit his barn at least twice a week. Sometimes it's to visit Susan, or as Bob would say, "Holding up the help." There are other times when I walk out to the barn just to visit him.

Ride on Bob

Love,
Your adopted horse kids
Bill and Susan

TABLE OF CONTENTS

FORWARD

To Kill A Horse is an entertaining novel with an innovative plot regarding the death of a valuable racing stallion, insurance fraud, a surprising murder and a budding love story.

Officer David Lowe of the Texas Department of Public Safety was about to retire from his job when he was sent to solve the death of the stallion after a wiretap was made by the FBI regarding the proposed killing.

Lowe, also a veterinarian who was raised on a ranch, was the perfect investigator as he was also friends with a horse trainer working out of the ranch, located in Whitesboro, Texas, where the killing was to take place.

Lowe enlists the help of the local Sheriff, the beautiful Marcia Selter, who was also a horse lover, and who made the job even more interesting.

The many twists and turns surprise the reader at every turn of the page as Chambers has the ability to bring you into the plot and not let you put the book down until the mystery has been solved.

-Glory Ann Kurtz

CHAPTER 1

TAKE THIS JOB

Officer David Lowe of the Texas Department of Public Safety was not a happy man. The job that he had once dreamed about as a child seemed to be an albatross hanging around his neck.

He could almost hear his grandfather Lowe in his ear. "Be careful what you wish for boy; you just might get it." The elder Lowe was no great fan of Texas Law Enforcement, blaming the department for his son's death when David was a young boy.

It wasn't always like that; not so long ago he loved his vocation. He was damn good at it. Uniquely trained in veterinarian medicine as well as law enforcement, Lowe was one of a kind. He was called "The animal cop" throughout the department.

He had lost his biggest supporter, his Captain. Captain Wade Wilson had been there ever since Lowe had graduated from the academy a decade earlier. Wilson was the only man he had ever had to answer to in his career.

"Your first Captain is a lot like your first love," Ranger Lucius Defoe had once told Lowe.

"Like your first love, you'll be hard pressed to find someone to measure up to your first commanding officer," Defoe added.

Captain Wade Wilson had been killed in a gun

battle with one of the Mexican drug cartels on the border. Officer David Lowe watched his beloved Captain be murdered under a smuggler's moon. He and Defoe had settled the score the old-fashion way but it didn't make him miss Wilson any less.

Lowe's new Captain, Terry McDowell, was all starch and not much soul. The man was nothing like his twin brother Gary, the Sheriff of Taylor County. Lowe had work a case with the Sheriff five years earlier. In Lowe's opinion, there might as well have been a cardboard cutout sitting behind Wilson's old desk.

Wilson had been gone for nearly nine months and Lowe doubted if McDowell had said fifty words to him. Everyday when Lowe arrived, there was always a mountain of paper work and a to-do list on his desk.

The only happiness that he found was that one day a week when he looked after the department's canine division and a parade string of ponies the DPS kept outside of town. Even then Lowe's new Captain required reports to be filed in triplicate.

Lowe mulled it all over day after day on his way into the office. However, it was a little different this particular day because he was forming a plan.

If it was true that the only happiness he could find were the rare moments when he was seeing after the department's critters, he might as well go into private practice. He'd make a hell of a lot more money. He had his grandfather's old horse place where Shawn Kelly, who was his oldest friend, had been training horses prior to the horse market hitting the skids. When that happened, Kelly had signed on with one of the bigger horse operations in North Texas.

Lowe's paternal grandfather, the man who had raised him, was among one of the elite in the cutting-horse world. You couldn't mention men like Chubby Turner or Bill Freeman without also mentioning Jonah Lowe.

David Lowe had grown up in the equine industry; he knew everyone who was anyone in that sphere. On the Lowe name alone, he knew he would have an instant client list the moment he hung out his shingle. Hard times or not, he knew he could make a go of it in the horse world.

Lowe thought about calling his old friend Shawn Kelly and seeing what his feelings were about him going into private practice. The two men had been close at one time, nearly like brothers. But over the years they lost touch. It was a damn shame but they just got caught up in life and forgot what was important. The thought of calling his old buddy and telling him about his new plan faded when he hit Austin traffic.

Ahead of Lowe was a three-quarter-ton, flatbed truck with a gooseneck stock trailer. Whoever was driving the vehicle seemed to be confused and possibly was drunk.

"I'll be damned, that's all I need this morning," he muttered to himself as he hit the lights. "More freaking paper work."

"Drivers license and proof of insurance," Lowe told the cowboy in the flatbed truck.

"Damn this town got big. I remember when it was just as easy to get around here as it was in Aspermont, Texas," the cowboy stated. "Then again, that was twenty years ago," he continued.

"Have you been drinking, Mr. McBride?" Lowe asked after reading the man's name off his driver's license.

"Not in a few years," he responded. "I promised my sister Sherry I wouldn't. Now my old dog Jester, who can say about him. He's been known to take a nip or two," the man said, joking and about that time a huge hundred-pound-plus dog rose up from where he was sleeping.

It didn't matter how bad of a day Lowe was having; the man's words made him laugh.

"Where is it that you're trying to get to, Mr. McBride," Lowe asked.

"Please call me Bubba Lee," was McBride's response. "I was supposed to meet my cousin at the Chuck Wagon Coffee Shop. He's a crusty old Texas Ranger and I'm gonna do my very best to sell him this rig then I'm out of here. Gonna get down to the islands and buy myself a boat. My days of pushing horns are done."

"What would be this Texas Ranger's name?" Lowe asked in a helpful voice.

"Lucius, Defoe," the cowboy's answered.

"I should have known when you said 'crusty,' that description fits Lucius like a glove," Lowe said with a laugh. "You just follow me; I'll show you the way."

Just who am I following?" the cowboy wanted to know.

"David Lowe," the officer answered.

"I'll be damned," McBride said holding out his hand. "Austin may be big but it's a small world. I went through boot camp with your daddy. He was a man among boys even then. It's a small world indeed little David."

The morning was starting to look up for Lowe but he still intended to tender his resignation as soon as he got to the office. Lowe decided he had time for a cup of coffee; after all it was Lucius Defoe and it had been a stretch of time in between their visits.

Defoe looked a bit gaunt and grayer since the last time Lowe had seen him. "Them damn bandits on the border are running me ragged boy," the old ranger fired back when Lowe asked about his health. "If you had my caseload, you wouldn't look too spry yourself."

Lowe could tell Defoe wasn't being completely straight with him about his appearance but who was he to question the man who wore the Cinco Peso pinned to his chest. The two names that always came up, when speaking of the best of the best in Texas law enforcement, were H. Joaquin Jackson and Ranger Lucius Defoe. They had spent so much time on the border that they were half Mexican themselves.

Defoe seemed to be his same jovial self despite his appearance. It wasn't long before he had Lowe rolling in laughter.

"You want to do what Bubba? Have you lost your mind? Here you come from one the oldest ranching families and you want to go to sea. I believe you've been watching a little too much 'Popeye the Sailor Man,' or listening to too damn much Buffett. Boy I think you're nuts. But who in the hell am I to stand in the way of your dream?" The old ranger could not help ribbing his kin.

"I'll buy your rig. But if you figure out them dolphins ain't as easy to rope as them shorthorns, come on home and I'll sell your rig back to you. Does that dog of yours come with the deal?" asked Defoe.

"Hell no, not at any price," the cowboy said with apparent disgust. "Old Jester is going to be my first mate,"

"That's a good thing," Defoe fired back. "I know that mutt and I couldn't afford to keep him in whiskey."

The conversation then went from the topic of Bubba Lee's up-coming adventure to Lowe's late father. Lowe had heard a lot of stories about his daddy. His grandfathers on both sides spoke highly of the man he barely remembered. He had been put to bed many a night with a tale about the man who gave his life for the great state of Texas. His mother had been taken in the very same bomb blast.

Later on in life, Defoe would tell him about the man he considered to be his best friend. The two men had been running buddies and "hell-raising sons of bitches" when they weren't on patrol. Defoe told him it was Lowe's mother who slowed the two down.

"If not for your momma, we likely would have ended up on the other side of the crossbars or under a headstone somewhere," Defoe had once confessed.

The fact was that because Lowe was so young at the time of his father's death, he knew him mainly through the accounts of others. He had obtained the stories of the elder Lowe's younger years from his grandfather. The later years, when he was a cop, Defoe had filled in the time frame. It seemed the only years that were missing were the ones when David Lowe Sr. had worn the patch of an army ranger.

Fate, or some other abstract reason, had brought this zany, sea-minded cowboy into Lowe's realm, maybe for no other reason than to fill in the lost years of his father's life.

"Like me, your daddy really stood out that first day at basic training," reminisced McBride. "We were the only two who showed up already with buzz cuts; you might say because of our roots, that's how we rolled. It didn't take long for our drill instructor to make all of them long haired city boys look like me and your daddy.

"The next few weeks they ran the dog out of us. I never understood why there was so much running involved. Hell it seems to me that you want fighting men, not runners," McBride said laughing while he took a sip of coffee.

"It was in the second week that the powers-to-be put your daddy over the rest of us numbskulls. A lesser man would have let that shit go to his head, but not your old man. Recruit Lowe had no 'ass-kissing' in him; it was all about help getting the rest of us ready for war. Make no mistake about it; we all knew that's exactly where we were headed.

"Before we graduated from boot camp, they let us go into town on a week-end pass. Them buzz-cut city boys hit the local bars and sporting houses like locusts. Your daddy and I heard there was a rodeo in town and we went to have a look-see. David thought I had lost my mind when I entered the bull-riding competition and he really thought I'd lost it when I told him to bet on me.

"I neglected to tell your daddy that I had made my living as a twister a year before Uncle Sam came a calling. Needless to say, your daddy and I were the only two who made it back to post with more scratch than we left with," continued McBride.

"A few days later, we received our marching orders. All, with the exception of your daddy, were sent to 'Nam. David would get there eventually after completing ranger school. Later I heard your old man graduated at the top of his ranger class. His prize: a first-class ticket to the shit.

"Let me tell you something son, them army rangers were some mean mothers. There is no telling how much time they spent behind enemy lines. It's just one of many dirty secrets Uncle Sam will never tell.

"I know this because in my second tour, my platoon was ordered to help liberate a POW camp in Cambodia. Who else would show up to lead the charge? None other than First Sergeant David Lowe. By then we held the same rank but he was miles ahead of me when it came to soldiering.

"We came on the camp at dawn. There were nine other men besides your daddy and me. The intell' we had been given wasn't even close. We were told there were no more then a dozen North Vietnamese guarding the camp. In the early morning hours, we must have counted fifty from our vantage point. Your daddy and I decided there was no going back empty handed.

"We knew we had to come up with something to tell our men: a battle cry if you will. David looked at me hoping I might have a story or something. All I could come up with is the story of the Comanche: 'Well men, the Cavalry chased the Comanche across Texas thinking there were millions of them. Come to find out, there were very few of them. But for years, they terrified the settlers. They were wild, loud and ruthless. If we are going to take it to

Charlie, we're going have to become Comanche warriors.'

'We came down the mountain hooting and yelling in a way that would have made Quanah Parker proud. Charlie didn't know rather to 'shit or get.' It must have been a sight.

"In the end, we killed every one of our brothers' captors. We knew it would be hard enough to hump it through the jungle with the malnourished prisoners. We had no desire in trying to do so with captives of our own.

'It's a medal you won't find in your daddy's things. According to the army, we were never there. But to those POWs, they'll never forget the day your old man led a crazy-ass outfit into that camp and saved their lives from certain death.'

McBride ended his war story saying, "When it comes to David Lowe Sr., you have a lot to be proud of."

The intent look on the cowboy's face told the younger Lowe that it was no bullshit story. Men who had experienced war firsthand rarely talked about it; when they did, you better take it as gospel.

Lowe swelled up with pride inside when he heard how his father had saved the POWs. He had no idea that when he had stopped the lost cowboy, the end result would be a story about a hero that just happened to be his father.

His coffee was gone and the two other men started to dicker over the price of McBride's rig. It was time that he headed into the office - for better or worse.

He thought about telling Defoe about his plan to resign from the force before he left but decided against it. He might have clued the Texas Ranger in if they had been alone but McBride changed everything. It might be better to tell his old friend after the fact. He was sure the ranger would try to talk him out of it.

He picked up the check and said his goodbyes while the other two men went back and forth on a price for the rig. It was a comical dance played out everyday somewhere in Texas. He had watched his grandfather Lowe do the same many times over a horse, usually with his best friend and noted horseman, Bob Kurtz. Once he had seen the two men dicker over a bale of hay.

"It ain't the price that matters boy, it is the thrill of the dicker," Jonah Lowe had once told his grandson after a session with Kurtz.

He wasn't thinking about the chore at hand as he drove, rather his mind was on the story McBride had told about his father. Lowe could only come up with one conclusion: his father had lived as a hero and died as one.

Lowe's thoughts of his late father were dashed as soon as he caught sight of the stack of paperwork awaiting his arrival. The anger and resentment he had felt earlier began to bubble up once more. He turned his computer on with a defiant grace in his movement. He began to pen his "Take-this-job-and shove-it" letter as soon as the damn thing booted itself up.

Lowe was almost ready to push the send button when a voice broke his train of thought.

"Hey Lowe, the Captain wants to see you," another DPS officer called out.

"Good, 'cause I have a thing or two I'd like to say in person," Lowe said to himself.

He thought about going ahead and sending the e-mail but decided to do the deed in person.

Captain McDowell was on the phone when Lowe knocked on his door. "Come in and have a seat. I'll be right with you," McDowell instructed as he put his hand over the receiver.

With the Captain being on the phone, it gave Lowe the chance to think about exactly what he wanted to say. He had been taught from an early age to respect authority and burning bridges might not be such a good thing. In short, his head had regained the argument from his heart.

"Lowe I know riding the pine hasn't been easy on you these last six months," said Captain McDowell, beginning the conversation. "All the accounts I've heard, say you're a damn good cop.

"The little fiasco down on the border ruffled some feathers that were above my pay grade. The political powers that be wanted their pound of flesh. Your ranger running buddy was a decorated veteran of over twenty years. As they say in the army, 'Shit rolls down hill.' It was everything I could do just to keep you on the force." A pause followed the Captain's explanation

"I probably should have asked this question awhile back but off the record, Just what and the hell did you and Defoe do to piss so many people off?" McDowell asked.

Officer Lowe saw something in McDowell he hadn't seen before. The look in the man's face and the sound in his voice said he was human after all. More than that, it said he could be trusted.

Lowe told him the story, at least the modern day story, of Geronimo's Ghost Ponies: The four-legged haunts were nothing but a ploy for the drug traffickers to get the product across the Mexican-American border. Raul Sanchez, a noted drug lord of the area was behind the plot.

Lowe told how he and Defoe had stumbled on to the smuggling operation. He then told how they had set up surveillance and how they had a pretty good idea when the smugglers would make their next run.

But it all went south after that; Lowe's beloved Captain Wilson had been killed when a crooked DEA agent interrupted the party.

Defoe figured out the Fed was dirty and set out to prove it. Lowe lightly skimmed over that portion of the story as some things were better left unsaid.

The DPS officer told a good story but it wasn't anything McDowell hadn't read in the report. It still didn't tell the reason why the brass had came down so hard.

"Son, like I said, this is just between you and me," said McDowell prodding for more of an explanation. "There has to be more than that to the story."

Lowe thought for a moment before answering. The Captain was right when he said there was more to it. Lowe just wasn't real sure how far he wanted to go out on a limb. He then decided to throw caution to the wind a let it rip. He figured "what the hell;" he was nearly out the door anyway.

"Well sir, we kinda set that dirty DEA agent up," explained Lowe. "We had the man who killed Captain Wilson in custody and he was fixing to roll on the Fed. Defoe carried the killer's sorry ass back to the scene of the crime while me and a local Sheriff kept our eyes on the dirty Fed. Sure enough the Fed fell for the bait.

"We didn't know he would take it to the extreme. Defoe's suspect was filling him in one minute and stone cold dead the next. The DEA agent had gotten a step on us and shot the man. By the time we got there, he was trying to do the same to Ranger Defoe. We took a few shots at him before he crossed the river into Mexico.

Come to find out, the suspect the Fed laid low was the nephew of Raul Sanchez, himself. It didn't take long for the news to get out about who shot who and get back to the boy's uncle. Not long after that, the DEA agent's body was found in that same river he crossed to get away from us," Lowe told his new Captain.

"And neither you nor Defoe knew the suspect was Sanchez's kin?" the Captain asked.

"No sir," Lowe said with a wink.

"It still doesn't explain how you two managed to piss so many off," McDowell said, trying to get a reason out of Lowe.

"Sir you have to look at the context this whole drama played itself out in. Six months earlier was the mother of all screw-ups in Waco. The last thing Washington needed was more bad press. They tried their best to make it appear like the dirt-bag died in the line of duty.

"Picture this sir: the same S.O.B. who got my Captain killed was going to be buried with the same honors. Some wouldn't stand for it and leaked the report to the press."

With that, Lowe ended his side of the story.

"I guess that would do the trick," said a surprised Captain. "Damn fools will never learn that the cover-up is always worse than the deed itself. As your Captain, I would tell you that what you did was the stupidest thing a man under my command could do and you're damn lucky you still have your badge. As a fellow peace officer, I would say, 'Good for you.'"

Those were the last words the two would ever say about the matter.

"Ain't it funny Officer Lowe how the worm turns sometimes?" Captain McDowell asked.

"How so sir?" Lowe asked.

"I just got off the phone with Washington. It seems like the sons-of-bitches who were so hot for me to can you, are now in need of your unique talents," McDowell explained to his officer.

The utter confusion of the moment left Lowe speechless. He went back to his desk and looked at the calendar to make sure there wasn't a full moon or that it wasn't Friday the Thirteenth.

Lowe could only guess that McDowell saw the strange look on his face when he started from the beginning.

"Have you ever heard the name Jackson Pride?" the Captain wanted to know.

"He's the fellow on the FBI's 'Most Wanted' list," said Lowe. "Dr. Death is what they call him. I've read a few articles about the scam artist. Seems he's a man with more than one con. He started being known for seducing elderly rich ladies and convincing them to purchase no-account racehorses at top dollar.

"He had another deal to offer once their racing careers didn't pan out. If they would split the insurance money with him, he would make sure the worthless nags meet an untimely death. Pride was making money both coming and going.

"But it all went south when he tangled with a victim that was on to him. The lady was heir to some candy fortune. I guess she asked one too many questions and she disappeared. All eyes turned to Pride and he pulled a vanishing act, landing on the FBI's shit list.

"Since then he's been something like a hired gun linked to several insurance frauds. If you have a stud shooting blanks or a horse not measuring up, Jackson Pride is the man you want to call," Lowe finished, filling his Captain in on what he knew about the case.

"Damn Lowe, so much for me getting you up to speed. You are really well read on this matter," McDowell stated.

"Well sir, people like Pride really get under my skin. I guess it's the vet coming out in me," Lowe explained.

"David, it seems the Feds caught this guy on a wiretap. He was planning on visiting our fair state and conducting a little deadly business," the Captain told Lowe.

"What do you mean, 'was'?" a curious Lowe wanted to know.

"It seems Mr. Pride is one slippery bastard. He figured out the Feds were on to him and made other traveling arrangements," said the Captain.

"Captain I am confused, what does all this have to do with me?" Questioned Lowe. "It seems plausible to enlist our help if Pride was headed this way, but since he is in the wind...." Lowe said, leaving his statement hanging.

"The FBI, along with the rest of the alphabet soup, has their hands full with the bombing of the federal building in Oklahoma City. It's really gotten nasty out there. Who would have ever guessed there were so many freaking wing nuts among the American population?" said the Captain.

"At any rate, they want us to look into it. Just because Pride has gone underground doesn't mean these folks won't still try to knock off the horse for the insurance money. Besides all that, it seems like perfect timing to get you back in the game," continued the Captain with a smile.

Ten minutes into the conversation, Officer Lowe had forgotten all about private practice and was telling the Captain what he could do with the job. He could see that his new Captain had just as much faith in his abilities as Captain Wilson.

Lowe's ears perked up when McDowell began to go over the particulars of the case with him. A little was due to the fact that he actually had a case but most of his interest came in the name of the ranch under suspicion.

"I understand you come from the horse world," said the Captain. "Have you ever heard of the Double D Ranch in Whitesboro?" he asked.

Lowe knew of the ranch because it was where Shawn Kelly had landed. Yet the fact someone would knowingly kill a good cutting horse for the cash was dumbfounding. The fact Shawn Kelly might be a party to it was something Lowe would never believe.

"Captain are you sure the Feds gave you the right name?" asked Lowe. "I grew up with the trainer on that place and I would stake my career that he wouldn't have anything to do with a scam like that," Lowe protested.

"I always thought you grew up in Texas, Lowe," said the Captain.

"I did," the confused officer fired back.

"Well it says here that Ed Thompson is from upstate New York," said McDowell, reading from the report in his hand.

"Who the hell is Ed Thompson?" Lowe asked, beginning to wonder what was going on.

McDowell gave Lowe the file that had been provided by the FBI. The officer began to intently scan the report.

"This will teach me not to stay in touch," Lowe committed after he finished looking at the report.

"I was not aware they had taken on a few racehorses. My friend that I was telling you about trains performance horses. It's my guess that one trainer does not know, or care to know, what the other is doing," Lowe explained.

"There you go Lowe, your ticket into the case," the Captain said with a smile. "You come up with line of attack, and we'll go over it tomorrow morning," McDowell told his officer.

Two actions were rippling through the being of Officer David Lowe: his step had more energy and each movement had a meaningful purpose. It wasn't like it had been the previous six months. His case of "drag ass" was gone.

The wheels in his head were also turning and a plan was forming. The plan was beginning to center around his relationship with Shawn Kelly. It was a call he would have to be careful with. He didn't want it to look like he was using his oldest friend. It was a call he would make after his daily shift was over.

CHAPTER 2

A NIGHT AT SHINOLA'S

Just like a faceless bandit, the virus first appeared in a woman in 1937. It was named for the region it was discovered in: the West Nile district of Uganda. The virus then vanished like some outlaw who had just held up the stage to Yuma. Like all "Most Wanted," the West Nile Virus couldn't stay hidden. Some twenty years later, the virus was back with a vengeance. In 1957 an outbreak hit Israel and those ravaged were among Israel's elderly.

The virus's trail would branch out from there, moving from Africa to Europe, then the Middle East and Central Asia. At the end of the twentieth century, the virus washed up on the shores of North America. The common denominator or "sidekick," if you will, was the mosquito. If the analogy is correct, then the mosquito acted like a six-shooter while the virus was like the bullet.

The West Nile Virus can cause severe meningitis or encephalitis. In other words, it causes swelling of the brain and spinal cord. The virus cannot only be contracted by humans, but also animals; most notably horses.

In the late 1990s, not a lot was known about the virus in either horses or human beings and when not a lot is known, panic sets in. If, as was first thought, the virus was transferred from bird to mosquitoes, then it was a short leap to think that humans could catch the virus from their horses. Since then science has proven that not to be the case.

It was in the West Nile Virus Panic in Texas that Officer David Lowe would make his move. The panic itself would provide the perfect cover for his investigation into the insurance scam.

Lowe conferred with noted equine disease specialist Dr. Grey from Oklahoma City before running his idea by his Captain. He then contacted the ranches and local veterinarians around the Whitesboro area after receiving his Captain's blessing.

Posing as a federal agent with the disease control office of CDC, Lowe instructed locals to contact him in the advent of an untimely demise of a horse. He also told them that failure to do so could result in prosecution as a federal offense.

A week after receiving his first case in months, Lowe sat looking up at the sign of a restaurant in Springtown, Texas. "Shinola's" was the name the officer saw on the restaurant sign.

Springtown, Texas, lay some sixty miles due south of Whitesboro. It was also the agreed-on location for Lowe to meet up with his old running buddy, Shawn Kelly.

The idea of meeting Kelly so far from the center of Lowe's investigation was to not arouse the suspicion of those who might see the two men together. The undercover scam might not work if it were known the two men knew one another. Lowe also wanted to get the lay of the land before making his presence known.

"There's this new place in Springtown and son I'm talking about some good eats," Kelly said to Lowe a few days prior to their meeting. "You meet me there and we'll do us some catching up."

Officer Lowe didn't have to wait very long for his old friend to arrive. In his rear-view mirror, he caught sight of a three-quarter-ton Ford pickup truck pulling into the parking lot. He had to smile. It was the same truck he had seen him driving years earlier and the last truck Lowe's grandfather had bought.

"Some things never change," Lowe thought to himself.

To the officer's surprise; he noticed even though his friend's vehicle hadn't changed, his appearance had. The last time he saw Kelly, he had long, dark, curly locks around his ears that were as pretty as any horse's mane. The dark locks were gone and in their place was a shiny baldhead.

"You want to put a hat on that damn thing before you blind me with it, Shawn?" asked Lowe, not able to resist ragging on the man.

Lowe also noticed that as the night wore on, that Kelly's hair wasn't the only thing different about his friend. The fire and wildness that had gotten the two into so much trouble during their youth wasn't much more than a flicker. Lowe was not so quick to poke fun at him, as sadness seemed to have replaced the fire that once lived in the man's eyes. Without any other information, Lowe could only surmise it was the hard life of a horse trainer. He had sometimes seen the same longing in his grandfather's eyes.

However, Lowe only saw the sad look for a moment. Kelly's mood seemed to change as soon as he heard the remark about his hairless head.

"Son, it takes a bigger man to keep the hair wore off than it takes to grow it," Kelly said with a wink. "The little filly down at Miss Flow's keeps the top of my head as slick as a banker's hand shake."

The old friends sat down to a meal of chicken-fried steak, homemade yeast rolls, mashed potatoes, and sawmill gravy. The dinner conversation centered around the memories they had experienced during the prime of their lives.

"Damn Shawn, you didn't lie about the food here," Lowe said while pushing away his plate. "It has been sometime since I ate this good,"

"I don't intend to lie about food, horses, or whiskey," Kelly boasted.

"And women?" Lowe asked with a grin.

"Lie to a woman, hell yes. I figure a man that won't lie for a little female loving is batting for the other team," the longtime horse trainer mused.

"Speaking of whiskey, I have a bottle in the car. What do you say we go howl at the moon like we did twenty years, " Lowe suggested.

"David, do you like Clint Eastwood?" Kelly asked out of the blue.

"I guess! Why?" Lowe answered, doing his best to figure out what the movie star had to do with them having a drink.

"There's a line from Dirty Harry I seem to be quoting more and more: *A man's got to know his limitations*. The horses are getting younger and I'm getting older. I have five of them knot-heads to ride in the morning. You catch my drift?

"The walk down memory lane was great," Kelly explained, reading more into their little reunion. "But I know that's not the only reason you're here. As your grandfather was fond of saying, let's get down to the nut cutting. Got to get my beauty rest or one of those knot-heads might stomp my ass into the ground."

"I guess after all these years, you can pretty much read me like a book," reasoned Lowe. "You're right, part of this is pleasure and part of it is business, and we both know what business I am in. What can you tell me about your boss, John Brown?" Lowe asked as his demeanor changed.

"The King of Silicone," Kelly replied with a wry smile.

"You mean he's in the high-tech industry?" came Lowe's follow-up question.

"Not exactly! I mean he owns a number of strip clubs down on the coast and a few over in the Metroplex," Kelly informed his old friend.

"Can you tell me what he's like," Lowe asked.

"He is a dandy," responded Kelly. "Do you remember Teddy Johnson and how he was always impeccably dressed. No one in the cutting horse world ever outdid Teddy when it came to his appearance. Brown makes Teddy look like a hobo. He has J.W. Brooks up there in Arkansas making all his hundred-percent pure beaver hats. Clay, over at Rambling Trails, custom makes his full-quill Ostrich boots, and Clay makes a fine boot. From head to toe, the King of Silicon dresses the part.

"But Brown's dress is where the comparison stops with Teddy. I like Teddy, always have, but I have little use for men like John Brown. The man talks big like he is a real Texan but just a few words out of his mouth lets you know right away that he's from up north. The son of a bitch is as crooked as a dog's hind leg, I tell you. I wouldn't trust him as far as I could throw him," Kelly answered with a look of spite in his eyes.

"If you dislike the man so much, why do you work for him," Lowe said with a puzzled look.

"I have my reasons," was all Kelly said.

For a brief moment Lowe saw the same sadness he had seen earlier in his old friend's eyes. He wished that he knew the correct words to say or had the time to listen to but he was on a case.

" You said earlier that you have five head to ride in the morning," said Lowe. "Any of them wouldn't be racehorses would they?"

"Racehorses! If I had a clue about racehorses I would stop going to New Mexico twice a year and losing all my money betting on them," said Kelly. "There's racehorses on the ranch but not in my barn. Your grandfather would spin in his grave if he thought I had anything to do with racehorses," Kelly answered, trying to get his glass of iced tea refilled.

The young waitress filled both their glasses to the brim and then went on to tend to other customers. Both men sat in silence until she was gone, with the exception of thanking her for her service.

"Brown got too close to his product and married someone half his age. I guess he figured if he didn't buy her a few playthings to keep her busy, her eyes would start wandering," reasoned Kelly. "Racehorses seemed to fit her fancy and before you knew it, they had a new barn filled with Kentucky's finest.

"But his plan didn't work. She has her toys but her eyes still wander from time to time, if you know what I mean," Kelly said in a matter-of-fact way.

"So it's Brown who likes the cutting horses?" Lowe wondered out loud.

"Not a bit. That goofy bastard is afraid of horses - I shit you not. Nope. Years ago I started working with his first wife when I was still at your grandfather's place, said Kelly. "She loved her cutting horses and that woman could sit a saddle like you would not believe. Now I train for her teenage daughter. I'll be damned if she doesn't have her momma's way with horses."

Kelly seemed to brighten up when he spoke about the mother-and-daughter cutters.

"What happened to Brown's first wife?" seemed to be the next logical question for Lowe.

Lowe knew by the look on Kelly's face that that question was going to be a hard one to answer. He stammered briefly before saying softly, "They say she killed herself," was about all he could bring himself to say. Once again, Lowe could see sadness in the man's eyes.

Lowe could also hear the doubt in his friend's voice when it came to the cause of death. The cop in him wanted to follow up on Kelly's answer, but the human being in him said it was best left alone.

"What does all this have to do with the price of rice in China?" Kelly wondered using one of Lowe's grandfather's favorite sayings. Lowe had to smile cause it brought to mind so many forgotten memories of a life lived long ago.

"You ever hear of a man named Jackson Pride?" Lowe asked.

"Ain't he the feller going around scamming all those rich ladies and the killing off their horses for the insurance money? Asked Kelly. "The had an article on him in *Western Horseman Magazine* a few months back. Dr. Death is what they called him."

Lowe marveled at the response. It had been nearly the same answer he had given his Captain days earlier, right down to the source. It was easy to see that the same man had taught both of them.

"Damn, this is starting to add up," said Kelly, putting the full measure of the picture together. "Are you telling me Dr. Death is headed my direction, David?"

"I don't think so, I think the Feds scared him off. You have to ask yourself though, if someone was desperate enough to go looking for Pride….." Lowe left his statement hanging in the air like low fruit, easily picked.

"I hear what you're saying, David. If someone calls on the good doctor, they might be just desperate enough to try to pull it off on their own. All I can say is, 'Not in my barn.' I tend my own horses just like your grandfather taught both of us," Kelly exclaimed.

"Hell, I know that," said Lowe. "If I thought you had any part in this, we would not be having this conversation. All I am really asking is do you know of any horse on the ranch worth more dead than alive," said Lowe, trying to put his old friend at ease.

"Ain't but one that comes to mind," said a thoughtful Kelly. "Double Ds Delight. He is a big, red stud with bloodline out the ying-yang. But then again, that big son-of-a buck brings in a shit load of money in breeding fees. It wouldn't make sense to kill the golden goose. But very little on the Double D makes a hell of a lot of sense," Kelly surmised.

It was almost like Kelly was having a one-man conversation. He had always been like that. Lowe had forgotten how comical his old friend could be as he worked things through in his head and out loud.

Lowe wondered that if things were so crazy for his friend at the ranch, why did he stay? He knew it would do no good to repeat his earlier question so he decided to let sleeping dogs lie.

"Now don't get me wrong David, all things are possible on the good ole Double D Ranch," Kelly offered. "I pretty much keep to myself and stay in my barn. I speak very little to the other trainer, stuck-up S.O.B. that he his. But we share a stall boy who I know pretty well. Let me talk to him and I'll see what he knows."

"Do you know about how many mares he bred last season?" Lowe asked regarding the stallion.

"If I had to guess, I would say, pretty close to fifty," said Kelly, puzzled over the thought. "It ain't no chump change at twenty thousand a pop. That's what I am saying, it doesn't make a damn bit of sense."

"I see your point, but what if the stud is shooting blanks?" Lowe countered.

"It's possible but you know how things are and how hard it is to keep secrets on a ranch. You would think if a high-producing stud had lost the lead in his pencil, I would hear about it." With Kelly's answer, a short silence fell about the men.

Officer Lowe was going over the mental checklist in his head. He had to be certain he had covered all his bases before the night ended. He didn't know when or if a move would be made to take a horse out for the payoff, but when and if it did, he wanted to make sure he was on top of his game.

Kelly was also deep in thought, perhaps more so than his old friend. He was wondering if everything Lowe had conveyed to him was true, and if so, then how did he miss it. He had been on the Double D long enough to know how shady events could get. He also questioned whether or not he left his guard down. A few more thoughts seemed to hover over him to the point he didn't hear Lowe's last question.

"Damn son, did you lose more than your hair?" Lowe asked in a playful voice.

"It appears so! I'm sorry David. What was the question?" Kelly answered while coming out of his trance.

"I asked you what the local law was like in Whitesboro," Lowe said, repeating his question.

Lowe's first-hand experience told him it was always a good idea to see what the locals were like. Ninety-nine percent of the time, they were true to their office, but there was always that one percent. The dirty DEA agent he and Defoe had tangled with on the border proved that point.

"Believe it or not David, we have us a woman Sheriff and she is a looker," Kelly said with that old playful glint in his eye.

Lowe couldn't help but laugh. "Same old Shawn. I didn't asked what gender she was or how she looked. I asked what the Sheriff was like. You know, how she does her job," Lowe said with a chuckle.

"She's a damn sight better than the last ass-kissing, dip-stick Whitesboro had. David do you remember all the big horse places up on Highway 380 between Denton and Greenville? You know up there where Shorty use to live? The big-time developers came in overnight, offering big bucks for those places. Well, they all sold out and started building bigger and better places on Highway 377 and northward.

"The further north you go, the fancier the horse ranches became. The mica at the end of this equine rainbow is Whitesboro. Charlie Roberts, the Sheriff back then, just couldn't help himself. He had his nose buried so deep in them rich folk's ass, I am surprised he didn't suffocate," Kelly responded, filling his friend in on the current history of law enforcement in that part on North Texas.

"I'm game. If he didn't suffocate, then what happen to Shit Sniffing Charlie?" Lowe asked of his friend.

"Charlie forgot one important detail, to keep his hand out of the till. Even though Whitesboro is overrun with the likes of John Brown, it's hard to get those pesky reporters to write anything but the truth about the crooked bastards," Kelly proudly pointed out.

"So you are saying the new Sheriff can be trusted?" Lowe replied.

"Like she was your own sister," Kelly answered.

"That's good enough for me. I know you're just as sick of answering all theses questions as I am asking them. I think I pretty much got all I needed. Why don't we call it a night?" Lowe suggested.

"Wait a minute old buddy. Answering all these questions has giving me a powerful thrust. Didn't you say something a little earlier about a night cap?" Kelly hinted.

"I thought you had some colts to ride in the morning?" Lowe reminded him.

"Thanks for the reminder but at the moment, I don't give a shit. I'll pay for it tomorrow. Where'd you say you were staying?" Kelly said while laying a five-dollar tip on the table.

"They said I could use the bunkhouse at the Hanging Tree Ranch," Lowe told his friend.

"Does ole Bill still own that place?" was Kelly's next question.

"Still writing books too," Lowe replied.

"Hell, I figured Bill done run off with that woman who works at Tractor Supply," Kelly remarked.

"It's not from the lack of trying, Lowe said with a laugh. "Bill is a bit too hard-headed to give up."

"I'll tell you what. I'll drink and you drive," Kelly said inviting himself to go along. "We can pick up my old truck in the morning. If you don't mind me bunking in with you,"

"Hell, if we are going all in, why don't we see if that biker bar on Highway 199 is still open? You remember, the first bar you ever took me to?" asked Lowe, joking on their way to his truck.

"Remember? Hell, the next morning I thought the old man would fire me for sure," Kelly fired back. "It sure wasn't the smartest idea I ever had. Now some twenty-five years later, you want to go back. To hell with that idea, and you went to college and everything. Besides we might not get out as lucky as we did last time and we are both a little old to be in a bar-room brawl,"

"I guess what you are saying is that you would settle for a glass of Kentucky's best sour mash and a warm fire rather than a tattooed chick which might lead to a Harley chain up side your head," Lowe cracked.

"Exactly," came the cutting horse trainer's one-word answer.

It was about a twenty-minute drive from where the two friends had their dinner to the Hanging Tree Ranch. With time to kill and black top to eat up, they began to talk about the old days and their youth. Events that seemed so dire when they were unfolding seemed all too comical but such is life and one's retrospect.

The only story that didn't make the men laugh was about the day Jonah Lowe, David Lowe's grandfather, died. A kick from a fresh horse had sent the old horseman to that big round pen in the sky. A few years later his old friend Bob Kurtz joined him.

"I can close my eyes and nearly hear those two old farts haggling over a mare, each one trying to get the better of the other," Kelly said with sadness in his voice.

"Yep, and it's probably the same damn mare they dickered over for twenty years," Lowe added.

It wasn't the first time the two men had spoken of Jonah Lowe's death. It always seemed to David that Kelly was holding something back. He sometimes wondered if it wasn't his own transference. Lowe had always felt guilty that he wasn't there to hear his grandfather's last words. He had been in College Station studying for his finals when the call came.

Shawn Kelly was the one who saw the old man take his last breath. He was the last to hear the final words from the horse trainer's lips. It was the one day in Lowe's life that he wanted back, and the one he knew he could never obtain.

These were Lowe's thoughts as his old friend rambled on about days gone by. It left the DPS officer with a hole deep in his soul and he couldn't help but wonder if it was the reason why they hadn't kept it touch like they should have.

"Damn David, what did Bill do? Go into the donkey business?" Kelly asked, breaking Lowe's train of thought.

"He told me the other day he had more ass than a fat girl," said Lowe with a laugh. "I really didn't know what he meant until I pulled through the gate earlier and saw all these donkeys looking at me."

"Well, at least he didn't rename the place 'The Dumb Ass Ranch,' " was Kelly's thoughts on the choice of the writer's yard art.

The two men talked and put a hefty dent in a bottle of Jack before turning in. The fire burning in an old potbelly stove warmed their outsides while the whiskey did the same for their inners.

The fire slowly burned as the whiskey cast its spell. Once again Lowe and Kelly were young boys. The memories made long ago were dug up like a strong box of an outlaw's treasure. They were young again, if only for a while.

"Damn son, you gonna sleep all day," a voice said, shaking Lowe from his sleep.

"Hell Shawn, it's six in the morning," Lowe grumbled.

"That means half the morning is already wasted," said Kelly. "Come on, get up and take me to my truck. I got ponies to ride. That's if some damn fool hasn't killed them while I was gone," the horse trainer added.

"If they did, call me, I'll help you hang the sons-of-bitches," Lowe responded as he pulled on his boots.

The two men were parked beside Kelly's old truck within twenty minutes. No good-byes were spoken for none were needed.

"You want me to do anything?" Kelly asked.

"Keep your eyes and ears open. You see anything, call me," Lowe replied.

"And what will you be doing," Kelly asked.

"I need to see a man about a horse," was about all Lowe said.

CHAPTER 3

GET A ROPE

Officer David Lowe discovered one thing about himself while he sat in exile after the dust-up with the Feds; there couldn't be anything worse than being a pencil pusher. On the Double D Ranch case, he found out just how wrong he was. The one thing harder than being a pencil pusher was dealing with the silly bastards.

Three days of meeting with the insurance people about a possible case of fraud had one of Texas's finest pulling out his hair. At the rate he was going, he was going to be just as bald as his old friend, Shawn Kelly.

They were so caught up in the confidentiality bullshit that they were about to let someone screw them out of two-million bucks. Lowe was nearly to the point where he was going to let them take the hit.

Another bean counter sat across the desk from Lowe, trying in vain to explain what kind of jeopardy they'd be in by disclosing the file on the horse in question.

"Fine if you're fool enough to help on this case, and you don't mind throwing mega-cash away, then I'll pack up shop and go back to Austin," Lowe said as he finally blew his top. "But call me to testify when it all comes crashing down around your pointed heads. I'll tell the judge we could have made an air-tight case if you all would have helped."

The man's eyes were as big as silver dollars. Evidently no one had ever been that direct with him. Likewise, Lowe had never seen a person crawfish so quickly. The man nearly strained a nerve trying to get the file out of his desk.

"Officer Lowe, Mother Nature calls on us all and it's calling on me as we speak. Unfortunately, the men's room on this floor is under repair. I'll have to use the one in the lobby. You being an officer of the law, I suspect I can leave you alone without fear," the man said with a wink and a nod.

"Sir, that goes without saying," Lowe answered, getting the drift of the man's implication.

The man left the case file on his desk and excused himself from the room. Lowe waited for a moment before taking the file in hand. He wanted to make sure the man had enough time for plausible deniability.

Lowe opened the Brown file as soon as the coast was clear. He reached in his pocket for his pen and his note pad and began deciphering the information contained in the records on the horses covered by the company.

Queen's Brassiere, a three-year-old filly, and the stud Kelly had told him about were the only two listed. The name of the filly had Lowe wondering if John Brown named everything after that part of a woman's anatomy. He decided the man must have issues.

The filly had a ten-thousand-dollar policy on her. In Lowe's way of thinking, the amount on the filly was not worth the risk. Double Ds Delight was a totally different story. Up until Lowe saw it for himself, the amount of the policy was purely rumor. In big bold numbers, the policy read 1.3 million dollars in the event of the big, red horse's death.

On its face, it seemed to be a pretty straightforward policy. It took Lowe back to the early part of his career when he was undercover as the "track vet" when horse racing was new in Texas. Lowe had to sign off on a few of the policies in that capacity.

The document stated that John Brown had purchased the policy but he had named Joslyn Jean, his second wife, as the beneficiary. Under the circumstances, it was enough to raise suspicion but about who?

Brown could have been experiencing financial problems and saw the one-time lump sum of 1.3 million dollars as a way out. By putting the policy in his wife's name could've been a way to throw the suspicion away from him.

A bubble-headed, ex-stripper might not be so dumb after all. There could be a number of reasons why she might want the horse dead. In Lowe's thinking, Mr. and Mrs. Brown were the only two who had an interest in the fraud; therefore, they were Lowe's two suspects.

"Suspect" was the word that seemed to hang in the officer's throat. No crime had even been committed and yet he was looking at suspects. It was like going to the plate with nobody on the pitcher's mound. He had a bat but not a damn thing to swing at. Little did the peace officer know that the ride of twists and turns had just begun.

Lowe did the only thing he could do. He took a deeper look into the backgrounds of his main suspects. A crime may not have been committed but when and if it did, he would be ahead of the curve.

Lowe remembered every time he'd bring up high-tech crime fighting in the presence of Defoe, the old ranger's eyes would glaze over. Defoe said all that he needed to fight crime was a badge, a gun, and his own wits. He would match "smartness" with any scumbag in Texas and nine times out of ten, he'd win.

"What about that one time, Lucius?" Lowe once asked.

"Hell I'd shoot 'em, then I'd let our Maker sort it out," the gruff old ranger joked in a way that left Lowe wondering if the Texas lawman was joking at all.

Lowe could drive all the way back to Austin and run the records of his that dub his "almost" suspects. It was an option, but he wanted to stay close just in case the call came in. Two modern technical advances would help him do both: a laptop and Google.

John Brown's name came up on a number of web sites, most in the adult-entertainment industry. Lowe couldn't help but wonder how the King of Silicon ended up in the middle of the Bible Belt. He then remembered what Kelly had said on that night they had spent drinking.

"Hell son, there are very few of us left there from Texas. It's a melting pot of the elite horse world from the East Coast, the West Coast, as well as other countries, Kelly said, slurring over his cocktail. "Hell, there's nearly as many Canadians in Whitesboro as there is in Alberta. Now don't get me wrong son, the more the merrier, but us Texans are damn sure out numbered,."

John Brown owned twelve high-end strip clubs on the Texas coast and a few in the Dallas-Fort Worth area. He also held an interest in a few other adult-related businesses in Lubbock and San Antonio. All in all, John Brown was worth millions on paper. The 1.3-million-dollar policy on the red stud seemed like a drop in the bucket.

Lowe could only trace Brown's life back about fifteen years and then it just stopped. It seemed like the man did not exist before that. It was hardly enough to raise suspicion, not really. Google itself hadn't been around that long. It was not enough to be the end-all.

Lowe remembered his friend mentioning the apparent suicide of the first Mrs. Brown. There was something in Kelly's voice that stuck with him. He'd have to research it more when he could find some access to the police database. Perhaps, when he paid the female Sheriff in Whitesboro a visit.

Lowe was in need of a cup of coffee before he Googled his last suspect. He thought of the place he had been hearing about: Starbucks. It was all the rage, opening new stores across the country. Dallas was one of the top ten cities in the U.S. so surely they would have one of the new-fangled coffee houses.

One hour later, he was sitting in a plastic chair, sipping on some exotic blend and about to Google the number two suspect of a crime he was still waiting for.

Joslyn Jean (aka JJ) Brown was different from her husband. It seemed to the DPS Officer that the woman's entire life was just a mouse click away.

Joslyn was born into poverty in the Piney Woods of East Texas. She was the second child in a family of eight and her father was killed in a bar fight soon after the last child was born. Her mother supported her brood the best way she could: selling pot in the trailer park where they lived.

By all accounts, Joslyn should have followed in her mother's footsteps by yelling at two or three dirty-faced kids, holding a baby, with a cigarette hanging out the corner of her mouth. The young girl was smarter than that and pulled herself up by her bra straps, so to speak.

She left home as soon as she graduated from high school. She put herself through college by waiting tables. She began a career in journalism by writing obituaries for a Houston newspaper.

One night, on a dare, she entered a talent contest at a strip club. The blonde-haired, blue-eyed bombshell won hands down. Joslyn discovered that she made more money in a two-hour span than she had earned in a month working at the paper. The dye was cast and the exotic dancer JJ was born.

Lowe couldn't help but find the humanistic and yet tragic telling of the woman's life interesting. It read like a novel you didn't want your friends knowing you were reading. All the twists and turns in her life held the DPS officer spellbound.

The seediness of her profession led her down the dark path of addiction, as it had for a number of dancers. It is an unspoken rule on the stage: "A stripper must use to dance and dance to use."

Just about the time JJ was circling the drain for the last time, she met John Brown at one of his clubs. The two found something in one another they hadn't found in anyone else.

The beautiful, twenty-something Joslyn made the middle-aged John Brown feel young and masculine again. She turned the heads of the men in his clique when she was on his arm.

"An alpha male in a jungle of wimps" is how he once described the almost drug-like high he felt when he was with her.

She had her own reasons for being with a man twice her age, none of which had to do with love. By that time, the emotion was more or less a whimsical dream she had left for dead in that dingy trailer park she had grown up in.

A man with the means of John Brown had the unique ability to take her away from the life she had grown to hate. Was he a knight in shining armor? Well maybe not, but a person who could offer her the security she had never known before? Absolutely.

In the end, this May-through-December relationship was part an American fairytale and part hillbilly tragedy. The law enforcement officer could glean no knowledge about her pertaining to his case, but all in all, it was a good read.

Lowe finished his over-priced cup of coffee and shut his laptop on his two prime suspects.

The next morning, he put in a call to the Sheriff who had Whitesboro in her jurisdiction. Lowe asked the soft voice on the other end of the line if she would meet him in Denton for a lunch.

He still wanted to keep his distance from the Double D Ranch and not blow his cover in case he needed to use it. Sheriff Marcia Selter, agreed to meet him later that day.

David Lowe's mind was a million miles away from the case at hand. The Sheriff's voice on the phone had sparked his interest. It was the soft and tender way the woman had. He wondered if the impossible was actually possible. Could the person on the other end of the line be as beautiful as the sound of her voice was? His logic told him that was rarely the case.

"What the hell am I thinking?" he said out loud. "I am on a case. Damn you Shawn Kelly for ever putting such nonsense into my head."

Questioning what he was thinking about the woman's voice didn't stop him from thinking of her. He just couldn't seem to help himself. Lowe tried to direct his thoughts to the case at hand but his mind would slip back to the female Sheriff. But he rationalized it by saying to himself that he didn't seem to have much of a case anyway. Not then anyway. Perhaps if he did, his thoughts might stay where he intended them to be.

So the DPS officer went up Interstate 35 toward Denton, Texas, with the sweet sounds of the woman's voice still ringing in his ear.

Sheriff Selter might have looked the part of a Texas belle, with long-brown hair, deep-green eyes and a frame that could stop traffic. But looks were as far as it went.

The Sheriff had joined the Marine Corp right out of high school and did a tour of duty during Desert Storm. Her service was so noteworthy that the Feds came calling. Selter was the youngest field agent ever in the storied history of the Secret Service at age twenty-four. She had spent five of her ten-year career undercover, infiltrating a South American counterfeit ring.

The stress of the assignment led her to early retirement and a twenty-acre piece of land in North Texas. She found the release from her stress in a string of barrel-racing ponies. She was more than content with the quiet life she was building for herself, for awhile.

A few articles about the at-that-time local Sheriff began to appear in the *Dallas Morning News*. No one could figure out how he was affording his lifestyle on such a modest income. An audit ensued and found the money in the jail fund had been raided. The leaders of the county were given a black eye when the Texas Rangers hauled away their sheriff in handcuffs.

The secret about Selter's background soon leaked out and the county officials came calling with hats in hand. It seemed to be a perfect fit because by that time, she was becoming bored with the female-dominated, barrel-racing world. For better or worse, she had lived her entire adult life in the sphere of men and she missed the challenge of that sphere.

It took very little for her to win her first term and even less for her second. It was no secret she ran a tight ship. Unlike the previous administration, she treated everyone the same regardless of their station in life. In doing so, she brought respect and dignity back to the office.

Lowe waited for the sheriff at a little Mexican food place just off the Interstate. It wasn't hard to pick her out when she arrived, not with a colt forty-five on her hip. And yes, Sheriff Marcia Selter was just as pretty as she sounded on the phone.

Lowe rose from his seat when she was shown to his table. He tipped his hat slightly, as was the custom he had been taught.

"I am officer David Lowe," he said when introducing himself.

"Of course you are silly. You're the only one besides myself with a badge," Selter couldn't help but saying with a smile.

She was full of piss and vinegar that was for sure and he liked that about her right off the bat.

"I've heard of you, officer Lowe. You are kinda like an urban legend in law-enforcement circles. Is it true you're a vet?" she asked.

"Yes ma'am," he answered.

"Peace officer and a veterinarian to boot," she exclaimed.

"Yes ma'am, I can write you a ticket and give your horse his shots at the same time," Lowe said jokingly.

It was clear from the get go, both Sheriff Selter and Officer Lowe had the same open personalities. It was also plain to see there was a little flirtation happening. The attraction was there but there was business at hand. Officer David Lowe was top-shelf in that department.

"I was taught to inform local law enforcement when running a operation in their jurisdiction," Lowe began after the waitress brought their drinks and took their orders.

"I appreciate the professional consideration. Now tell me what one of my residents has gotten themselves into," she formally asked.

"Well, so far nothing although the risk is high that there will be a fraud committed," he answered.

"I can deduce from your presence that it has to do with livestock in one form or another," she responded. "Your unique qualifications bear that out."

"Pretty and smart," Lowe thought to himself.

Lowe began with the most logical point: the beginning. In his mind, the beginning was the wiretap the Feds had. He couldn't tell her exactly whose phone was tapped because he didn't have that information. Sheriff Selter seemed to understand. Lowe guessed that it was because she had once been a federal agent herself.

He spoke of how the notorious con-artist had been heard making a deal with someone related to the Double D Ranch. The Feds wouldn't release the tapes so he had no idea who the other party was.

The Feds weren't releasing a whole lot, like what had scared the flim-flam man off. He was almost certain the Feds had some skin in the game, but he didn't relay his concerns to the Sheriff. He thought that some things were best kept to himself.

Secondly, he went over knowledge he had gained from the underwriters at the insurance company.

"It was like pulling teeth with those bastard," he said, quickly apologizing for using the expletive.

"Officer Lowe, I spent a tour of duty in the Corp," said Selter. "I am sure there is nothing you could say I haven't heard or said myself," she told him trying to put him at ease.

"Well, there you have it. I realize it's not much to hang your hat on but it's all I have at the moment. Now it's just a waiting game," Lowe said as he finished telling the beautiful Sheriff what he knew.

"I have always found waiting the hardest part of law enforcement," she said in an understanding tone.

"I would be grateful for any knowledge you may have on the workings of the people at the Double D Ranch," he told her while trying to drag his lunch date out as long he could.

He and Kelly had already plowed that ground a week earlier. "Now who's playing the role of a con-man?" he asked himself.

He then reminded himself of what Kelly had once told him when they were younger men. "A man who won't use a little deceit to worm his way into a woman's heart, well hell son, he's batting for the other team." The memory of the quote brought a smile to his face.

"I don't know if I have ever seen Mr. Brown. I hear he spends most of his time away on business. Some say he is like a ghost. He's lived here for years without being seen," she continued.

"Mrs. Brown, she's a totally different story; she quit the social butterfly about town, dressed to the nines no matter if she's going to a gala or to the mailbox. She wears a year's worth of my salary anywhere and everywhere she goes. She's rich and she wants to make damn sure everyone knows it.

"The rumors swirl like dust in a West Texas gale about her love life; you know how small towns are. There isn't enough time in the day for her to have as many lovers as she is rumored having.

"I try to steer clear of such nonsense," said the Sheriff with a laugh. "My jail would be overrun if I arrested folks from what I hear in the coffee shop alone."

"Have you heard anything about the death of the first Mrs. Brown?" was the next question Lowe asked.

"Sure, when I first moved to this part of North Texas, that's all anybody talked about, answered Sheriff Salter. "In all my years of experience, I never realized there were so many ways to kill someone. Every other week a new theory was floated.

"It all seemed to stop with the coming of the new Mrs. John Brown. It was like the population had a new toy to play with. I guess for a while, the two interacted. You know, he killed his first wife for a newer, younger model. Her rumored sexual exploits seemed to be of more interest after awhile. You know how people are?" she stated

"Yes I do, but have you ever looked at the suicide report on the first Mrs. Brown. I do realize you were not in office when it happened, so please don't take offense," Lowe asked gracefully.

"No I haven't, but I don't know how much good that would do," she told him. "The previous administration wasn't real big on reports. I'll see if I can find it for you if you would like."

"I wouldn't mind looking at the report," said Lowe. "At least it would give me something to do until something happens. I have a meeting with my Captain tomorrow. He wants me to give him a once-over on the investigation so far.

"My plan is to get a motel room in Gainesville after that meeting. I'd like to be a little closer in case something breaks. I'll give you a call and let you know where I am staying. I'd like to keep my presence a secret for now, if you know what I mean," Lowe explained.

"Sure, that goes without saying," the Sheriff agreed.

They talked a bit more after they finished their lunch. He picked up and paid the check before walking the Sheriff to her car. In a way, it felt like a first date without the goodnight kiss.

"You keep me in the loop," she said to him.

"Will do. You have a safe trip back now, you hear," Lowe said while he was walking away.

It was a good thirty-minute drive back to the Hanging Tree Ranch where Lowe was staying. Even though his first encounter with the beautiful Sheriff was all about the case, he couldn't help replaying it over in his mind. Lowe would later say he was "hooked from the start."

It dawned on him about halfway back to the bunkhouse that he didn't ask Selter if she was seeing anyone special. But Lowe convinced himself it was not the time or the place.

Lowe left early the next morning for the Dallas-Fort Worth Metroplex. Captain McDowell was in town to give a lecture to some new recruits at the police academy in Ft. Worth. Both men thought it would be a good idea to meet while the Captain was visiting.

Lowe didn't want to get too far from Whitesboro in case the call came in. He could hop on Interstate 35 and be on location within forty-five minutes from Fort Worth, which was over three hours from headquarters in Austin.

Captain McDowell needed a progress report since the Feds had been badgering him for a week. It was only one of his reasons for the meeting. He finally got the powers-that-be to loosen up the purse strings enough to allow him to obtain a couple of cellphones for his people in the field.

It made perfect sense to him. After all, the bad guys were already utilizing the new technology. Good sense didn't carry a whole lot of weight when it came to the bean counters and the state legislature. They'd rather give the people a tax break than make sure the force was up to date. It was good for the politicians but not worth a damn for law enforcement.

A day earlier, the Captain asked Lowe where a good spot was for the two to meet. Lowe ask if he would mind meeting him at Will Rogers Coliseum off of University Avenue in Fort Worth. It seemed like a strange place to have a meeting but McDowell went with it.

Lowe met his Captain that morning at the entrance with a fresh cup of coffee for his commanding officer.

"Captain, have you ever seen any cutting?" Lowe wanted to know.

"No, but I really don't have the time to watch any now," a confused McDowell let it be known.

"Sure you do Captain. With what little I have to report, I can tell you during the first bunch of cows. My friend that works for the Double D Ranch is in the first bunch of cattle. I want to see what has been happening since last we spoke. Talking to him after he shows will not raise any suspicions," Lowe reasoned with the Captain.

Reluctantly the Captain gave in and followed Lowe inside. The men had to pass through the exhibit hall to get to the cutting arena.

The hall was filled with merchants selling anything and everything, from horse tack to furniture and decor. The Captain didn't know what he was more surprised about: that the cutting world even existed or that so many in it knew his officer.

"It's not so much me sir, it was my grandfather. He was a cutting horse trainer. I took my first steps in an exhibit hall just like the one we just left," Lowe explained.

Lowe began to tell McDowell what little progress he had made since last they spoke. Basically it was a slimmed-down version of what he had related to Sheriff Selter the day before. He did; however, leave out the part about finding her so attractive.

"That's it?" the Captain asked.

"Pretty much sir; about all I can do now is wait until I have a crime. If you want me to go back to Austin and work on some other cases, I can, but for now I have nothing," Lowe exclaimed.

"No, no. You better stay here," said the Captain. "We will give it another week. I've just got to figure out what I'm going to tell Washington; they've been all up in my ass for a progress report.

"Oh yes, I do have something for you," the Captain remembered, handing Lowe a small box.

"It's a cellphone; it might come in handy on this case. I've already had the geeks at headquarters program it for you. Any call you receive pertaining to the case ought to come straight to you," McDowell said.

Lowe did know what he was more shocked over: the cellphone or that the Captain actually used the word "geek".

They watched the last few riders in the bunch and then Lowe walked the Captain out to his car. McDowell told his officer to call him as soon as he got set up in Gainesville. Lowe said he would and then watched his Captain drive away.

Lowe walked directly back to the stalls in search of Kelly. He knew Kelly would be in a good mood because he had marked a good score for his two-and-a-half-minute run.

It wasn't going to be easy finding his old friend, as there were a lot of horse stalls at Will Rogers. However, luck was in his favor that day because he ran into Marvin, an old black man who helped manage the barns during cutting events.

He had known the old man ever since he was a small child. Marvin would watch the young boy while his grandfather showed his horses. Lowe knew, without a doubt, that the old man would know exactly where Kelly was.

"Boy I ain't seen you since your grandfather passed. It appears you've growed up straight and true," the old black man said with a twinkle in his eye.

"It's good to see you too, you old horse thief," Lowe kidded.

You haven't seen that no-good Shawn Kelly lurking around here have you?" Lowe said, getting down to the reason he was in the barn.

"You just missed him. He handed me his horse and said he was on his way to J & S Saddlery to look at some new 'butt leather.' That'd be in the Exhibit Hall young David. I don't reckon I can call you that anymore, now can I?" the old man said.

"Papa Marvin, you can call me anything you want," Lowe said, remembering what he used to call the man.

J & S Saddlery wasn't the easiest place to find when walking through the maze of venders. He found who he was looking for after a few minutes of walking up and down the isles.

Kelly started talking as soon as he saw Lowe. "Damn David, did you see my run? It was like your old grandfather was smiling down on me. It's been awhile since I had a ride like that, good enough to make the finals.

"Come here I want you to meet someone," Kelly said with an inviting tone.

"David, this is Jimmy Watson, a saddle maker from San Angelo. Jimmy, this here is my oldest living friend, Officer David Lowe, one of Texas's finest," Kelly said introducing the men.

"Damn, how many saddle makers does San Angelo have?" Lowe said shaking the man's hand. "I just talked to a man named Tim, another saddle maker from Angelo two rows over. Then there's Kenny Kerns on the other side of the Hall. When I was a kid, my grandfather had to go all the way to San Antonio to buy a new saddle. Now you can't throw a rock without hitting one,"

"Yes but Jimmy is the best," Kelly bragged.

"I don't know about that, I am just the only one that will give you credit. Tim is just a little smarter than me," said a joking Watson..

The men made small talk while Kelly tried one saddle and then another. Kelly then told the saddle maker he'd be back to get the one he had picked out.

"You thirsty? After a ride like that I could sure use a beer," Kelly declared.

"I'm on duty, Shawn. But I'll go with you," Lowe told his friend.

Lowe walked with Kelly over to the beer stand and paid for the man's brew. They then found a place to talk.

"I ain't seen nothing out of the ordinary," Kelly reported. "I have been keeping a close eye out," he added.

"I'm going to move my base of operation up to Gainesville this afternoon," said Lowe. "I'll call you and let you know where I'm staying. Here is my new cellphone number. You can reach me on it day or night," Lowe said as he took a pen from his pocket and jotted the number down.

"Look at you, all uptown with a cellphone. Next thing you know, you'll be on *Walker Texas Ranger* with Chuck Norris," Kelly joked as he slapping his knee.

"By the way, I had lunch yesterday with Sheriff Selter," said Lowe, but he knew as soon as he said it that he should have kept his trap shut.

"Ain't you the stud puppy?" Kelly teased. How did that go? Did you show her your new cellphone?"

"No, no. I just got the phone a few minutes ago. And our meeting was professional. But she is a looker, I'll give you that," Lowe said, trying to explain.

"That she is my friend, a looker with no ties as far as I know. And believe me, I consider myself somewhat of an expert on such matters," Kelly boasted.

"If you are so much of an expert on such matters, then why ain't she in your barn?" Lowe fired back.

"Well old buddy, there's something about a woman with a firearm that scares the shit out of me," the horse trainer explained.

"With good reasons I suspect," was Lowe's take on it.

They talked and joked for the better part of an hour before Kelly had to go turn back the cattle for a fellow cutter.

Lowe thought about watching another bunch of cattle before leaving but decided against it. He had miles to go and things to do before calling it a day. He did; however, make it a point to go back to the stalls to say his goodbyes to the old black man that he knew as a boy.

Lowe was awakened the next morning at his new digs by a phone call. "Get a rope," was all the voice said.

Having been in a deep sleep, it took a moment or two for it to register.

The voice was that of Shawn Kelly's. He then remembered the early morning conversation they had the week before when he said he would help Kelly hang anyone who killed a horse. He suddenly knew exactly what Kelly was saying. A horse had bit the dust on the Double D Ranch.

CHAPTER 4

TO KILL A HORSE

L owe's new cellphone never seemed to be more handy than the day the killing games began.

The Department of Public Safety officer was faced with a bit of a problem. He had received word that the stud horse in question was lying dead in his stall but he couldn't afford to make a move too soon.

According to Kelly, it was true that the racehorse had breathed his last, but a crime had yet to be committed. Lowe was chomping at the bit to get his real investigation underway and yet he had to wait for a call from the attending vet, which was called for by the directive he had sent out two weeks prior. Who ever perpetrated the senseless act would no doubt know something was up if he just magically appeared on the scene.

The notification by the vet was only half of the equation. It was enough to get him to the barn to examine the remains but not enough to call it a crime. Even if he could prove the animal had died by causes other than natural, it was not illegal to kill your own horse, no matter how terrible it might sound.

The second and all-important piece of the puzzle was the call to the insurance agency to place a claim against the policy. Placing the claim on the policy after killing the horse was the crime: the crime of fraud.

There was no doubt this was a tightrope that Lowe had to walk carefully. He had to be careful with every step he took, and for the moment, that meant he had to be patient and hope the vet would call.

Lowe had just finished shaving when he heard the ringing of his cellphone.

"Inspector Lowe," he answered using his undercover front.

"Yes Inspector Lowe, this is Dr. Jason Southerland up in Whitesboro. I have a male horse, about ten years of age, who has died during the night. I'm calling to comply with a memo I received from the CDC a few weeks back," the man said in an educated voice.

"I see Dr. Southerland. Normally I would have you take a blood sample and overnight it to our office but since I am about thirty minutes away from your location on another case, I'll come by personally and take care of it myself," Lowe answered, trying not to sound as excited as he was.

The man seemed a bit disjointed on finding out how close the so-called CDC inspector was to the Double D Ranch. Lowe could hear the pause in the man's voice but decided not to read much into it. It could have been his own unfamiliarity with his new cellular device for all he knew.

"You say you're about a half hour away. I tell you what Inspector, I'll just wait here at the barn for you," Southerland said and then gave him the directions to the ranch.

Lowe played along asking questions here and there. "I take a left off of 377 on to 82, right?" questioned Lowe. He knew full well where the Double D was located because he had driven past it the night before. He couldn't help himself, even though he knew he was taking a chance on being seen.

As he hung up the phone, Lowe was thinking that the first part of his equation had come together nicely. The second part came a few minutes later when the underwriter from the insurance company reach out and touched him. Mrs. Brown had called inquiring about how to navigate a claim on the policy.

Lowe thought, "There it was: the crime. There's a slip between a cup and a lip," as Jonah Lowe used to tell his grandson. There would be a few hurdles he would have to clear before he could make anything stick.

He put in a call of his own after hanging up from talking with the man from the insurance company.

"Sheriff Selter's office," came a voice on the other end of the line.

"Is the Sheriff in? This is Officer Lowe calling," he said.

"Is this the same, cute Officer Lowe that the Sheriff had lunch with a few days ago," the anything-but-shy, female voice asked.

"Give me that phone, Gracie," Lowe overheard in the background.

"I am so sorry, Officer Lowe," he then heard, along with the embarrassment in the Sheriff's tone.

"Call me David and don't worry about it. I have someone just like your Gracie in my life," Lowe told the Sheriff referring to Shawn Kelly.

"I'm sorry David, I haven't found that case file on the suicide of the first Mrs. Brown yet, but I am still looking for it," she said, thinking the old report was the reason why Lowe had called.

"That can wait. How fast do you think you can get us a warrant to search the Double D Ranch?" he asked

"I don't know but I do know an old judge who enjoys watching me walk away a little more than he should. Why? Do we have smoke," she asked about the case.

"Oh yes, and maybe a little fire," was Lowe's response.

"Just in case your charm isn't quite enough, let me give you my Captain's telephone number as well as the insurance underwriter's number. It ought to be enough to get a warrant from any judge.

I don't know how long this horse has been dead so time may not be on our side. I can look over the carcass and perhaps even find a cause of death but I can't take any tissue samples or take custody of the body without a warrant," Lowe explained.

"I Roger that, I'll meet you there as soon as possible," the Sheriff said in an understanding tone.

Five minutes after Lowe's conversation with the Sheriff, he was pulling through the entrance of the Double D Ranch. The gate bore two pink D's welded on the rot-iron slats.

A narrow, gravel lane went by the main house and then curved left to the barns. He saw a vet wagon parked in front of the first barn and knew X marked the spot. A tall man stood by the wagon and then walked out to meet Lowe.

"I am Dr. Southerland. You must be Lowe," the man said when introducing himself.

"That would be me. Have you examined the body yet?" Lowe answered not beating around the bush.

"No, I have been waiting on you arrival," Southerland offered.

Lowe thought the man's answer was a little strange. After all, he was the vet the owners called out. Perhaps he had worded his phony directive a bit too harshly, he thought.

"Well, let's go have a look," Lowe said getting his collection kit out of the trunk of his car.

Lowe had to be eight or nine years old when a bad thunderstorm blew up where he lived with his grandfather. Lightning was hitting all about the place and the horses in one barn were coming undone. It was as if they knew something bad was about to happen.

Jonah Lowe had trained horses for most of his life and learned to listen to them. "

"Do you smell that?" Lowe asked Southerland.

"Yes, what the hell is it," the vet asked putting his hand over his nose.

"Burned flesh, there's nothing in the world that smells like. I believe we can say without looking at the horse, West Nile is not the agent of death. The horse has been electrocuted. You mind if I have a look?" Lowe asked the vet.

"Knock yourself out. The horse probably spilled his water onto that plug end over there," the vet said pointing at an electrical cord running through the stall. "A freak accident," he added.

Lowe knelt down by the horse's head and opened his mouth. The tongue was badly burned, with some kind of prong leaving a deep impression. He then made his way to the back of the animal and examined its anis. It was like it had been blown out.

Lowe knew just by his quick once-over that it wasn't a freak accident that had killed Double Ds Delight. Someone had put a bare electrode to the horse's tongue. The voltage had passed through the body and shot out the rear. Lowe had never seen it firsthand before but he had read about the method.

"It must have been a hell of a way to die old fella," he whispered to the dead racehorse.

Lowe also saw traces of blood on the shavings that covered the floor of the stall. He thought the blood droppings were out of place. He couldn't see any wounds on the horse's body, and even if there were, the electrocution would have cauterized the lacerations.

"Well, what do the think?" Southerland asked.

"I think the horse is dead," Lowe said, stating the obvious.

"Freak accident, huh," the vet stated as though it was true.

"I don't think so, but I can tell you more in about thirty minutes, if you want to wait," Lowe said rising to his feet.

"Just who are you?" the vet asked in a suspicious tone.

"I'll tell you that when I tell you what killed this animal," Lowe fired back.

"I'm going to talk to the owner up at the main house. I would appreciate you waiting in your vehicle," Southerland told the undercover officer.

The suspicion in the vet's voice was thick and filled the air. Lowe knew then the gig was up. Southerland didn't know who he was but he was pretty sure he wasn't with the CDC.

Lowe didn't care at that point. He had been patiently waiting for three weeks for that day to come. He had a dead horse that had died at the hands of someone, he had the call in to the insurance adjuster and he had a warrant on the way. Lowe was feeling good about the situation as he walked out to his car. But that would be his first misstep.

Lowe busied himself by drawing out a diagram from memory of the stall while he awaited Sheriff Selter's arrival. He knew it would be an undertaking he would have to do anyway.

From the corner of his eye, he saw Shawn Kelly walking toward his car. He rolled down the window to greet him.

"Well?" was all that Kelly asked.

"Shawn, we can't be seen together right now. I thank you for the heads up but we've got to let it play out. I'll call you tonight and we'll grab a burger," "Lowe told his old friend.

"I'll be on pins and needles," Kelly said as he pushed away from the car.

Lowe went back to his task at hand. Ten minutes after Kelly had approached him, Lowe saw the Sheriff's car through his rear-view mirror pull in behind his. She gave him the thumbs up when he got out of his vehicle.

Selter had no sooner handed Lowe the warrant, when Southerland and Mrs. Brown came around the barn.

Southerland and the woman were walking at a fast rate. Lowe could detect she wasn't happy. But who is happy to see the cops with a warrant in their hand.

"Are you Mrs. Brown?" Lowe asked knowing full well she was.

"I am and I would like to know what business you and our good Sheriff have on my property?" she demanded to know.

71

"It's called fraud, Mrs. Brown. You have a dead horse that has been insured for a lot of money; a horse that was electrocuted, murdered if you will," Lowe pointed out.

Wait a damn minute. You are not a veterinarian. You can't say with just a once-over if the horse was purposely killed," Southerland protested.

"I beg to differ with you, Jason," Selter said, coming to Lowe's defense. "He is a veterinarian, and a highly respected one. He is also a Department of Public Safety Officer."

Lowe was beside himself at the way the Sheriff stood up for him. "I'd go into a shootout with her anytime," he later remembered saying to himself.

"Mrs. Brown, we have a warrant to search the ranch and collect evidence. So if you allow us to do our jobs, we will come talk to you when we are done," Lowe said trying to calm the situation.

"You think I killed my own horse? You're crazy. I loved that horse. Besides he is worth more to me alive than dead," the visibly upset woman said.

"Go ahead JJ, tell them what you told me up at the house," Southerland interrupted.

"I asked our stall hand to saddle D up for me to ride last evening. I don't know if the young man had been drinking or what. Whatever the reason was, he tried to kiss me. I fought him off but not before he grabbed at my breast. You see I still have a mark," she explained pulling down her shirt and revealing the top portion of her left breast.

"I think I hurt his ego worse than he hurt my breast. The next thing I know is he is cursing at me and telling me it was my fault," she said in tears. "I fired him right then and there. He stormed out of the barn swearing that, 'I hadn't heard the last of him and I would pay.' Then I wake up this morning and find D is dead, so I guess I did pay," she finished.

"What is the young man's name?" Lowe asked the woman.

"Garret. Garret Mise," Southerland answered for her.

"I'm sorry Mrs. Brown, but we are still going to enforce this warrant. If you would like to file charges on the Mise kid, we'll take the complaint as soon as we finish collecting the evidence," Lowe said in an understanding voice.

Southerland put his arm around his client to try to console her as they walked off toward the house.

"Where should we start?" the Sheriff asked Lowe.

"Guess I need to call my Captain first. We need to get someone out here to pick up the last remains of Double Ds Delight. I am going to do my best to get him sent to Texas A&M for an autopsy. I really don't have time to run this investigation and do one myself.

"Why do we need an autopsy? You said he was electrocuted," the Sheriff wanted to know.

"Well there's other things the autopsy can tell us about the overall health of the horse. She was right, if the horse was healthy, he was worth more alive than dead. The autopsy might give us a motive," Lowe explained.

"Are you buying her story," came the Sheriff's next question.

"I don't know, the mark on her breast was real enough. I just can't believe she pulled the thing out," Lowe said almost blushing.

"Hell, I can. She used to show those puppies off for a living. I'm not buying it, not for a second. If you asked me, she's probably the one who came on to him; that's if any of her story is true," Selter said, letting her suspicions be known.

"I can't argue with you there but what we think and what we can prove is a different story," said Lowe. "Until we gather the evidence and have it analyzed, her version is plausible," he stated.

"I know, but some times I wish it could be that easy," she confessed.

"That's why we get paid the big bucks," Lowe said with a laugh.

"I'll start dusting for prints around the horse's stall while you are talking with your Captain," Sheriff Selter offered.

"Roger that," Lowe replied while reaching for his cellphone.

"Captain, it's Lowe. Just calling to give you an update," he said when Captain McDowell answered.

Lowe went over everything he had discovered as of then. He told the Captain how easy it was to spot the cause of death, as well as his inner action with Southerland and Mrs. Brown and the explanation she offered. He then told his commanding officer about enlisting the help of the local Sheriff.

"Good job Lowe, I knew you were the man for the job. Now maybe I can get the Feds off my ass for a while. If there's anything I can do ….," The Captain left his words hanging like a fastball over the plate.

Lowe figured it was as good a time as any to take a swing.

"Captain, there are a few things I do need to ask of you. I need a truck with a reefer to come pick up the body ASAP. I would also like to send it to A&M because they do good work Sir. All I have to do is make the call. I feel like if they did the work-up, it would stand up in court a lot better than if I did it," the officer explained.

"I see your point, Lowe. I need you there anyway running the operation. I'll get on the horn and send you a truck. I am also sending a black and white to transfer the evidence you find to the crime lab. You just call when you are done processing the scene," Captain McDowell said like he was reading Lowe's mind.

Lowe put his rubber gloves on, grabbed his evidence collection kit and joined Sheriff Selter in the barn.

He found the Sheriff staring at the stall gate with a dumbfounded look on her face.

"Something have you stumped?" he asked walking toward her.

"How many times a day do you think this gate is opened and shut?" the Sheriff asked. "I know at my place, I'm in and out at least ten times a day."

"And that has you stumped?" Lowe questioned.

"No, not by itself. Wouldn't you think the gate would be plastered in prints? I only found one set, and I bet they belong to you," she surmised.

"It is just a little strange. I'll give you that," Lowe said, scratching his head.

"That's not the half of it," continued the Sheriff. "Look at the floor outside the stalls. There are bits of shavings, a little spilled feed, dust and what not. Everything you would expect to find in a horse barn. Now look in front of Double Ds Delight's stall. Nothing, not a particle of dirt," her words echoed in the barn.

"Just a little overkill, I agree," Lowe stated.

"I would say so. If the Mise kid did it the way they claimed, he's one smart cookie," the Sheriff said shaking her head.

"Either that or he watches entirely too much TV," Lowe added.

"How well do you know the Mise boy?" he asked after a measure of silence passed between the two.

"I've seen him around a few times. He seemed to be a quiet kid, a good-looking boy. You know, kind of scruffy," she answered.

"What is it about scruffy, you ladies find so appealing?" Lowe joked in the middle of collecting evidence.

The two peace officers worked side by side for the better part of the afternoon. Lowe collected evidence in the stall and took samples from the dead horse. The Sheriff worked the barn area looking for other traces of evidence. The conversation was light - mostly about themselves.

Lowe found out that the Sheriff had grown up in a small town in Kentucky. Her father was a tobacco farmer and a small-time horse trader. She said it was through him that she found her love for horses. No matter where she was, she had always kept a horse.

Selter talked about the fact that even though she loved her family, she couldn't wait to get out of the backwardness of the hills of Kentucky. She gave it as her reason for joining the Corp.

"I spent some time in your fair state right after I joined the force," Lowe told her. "My first Captain and the Governor sent me up there to study the dark side of horse racing. I spent a few years as an undercover racetrack vet when Texas opened the first tracks. I thought Kentucky was about the prettiest place I'd ever seen."

"Yes, but there's miles of difference from where I was raised and the paved streets of Lexington," Selter responded.

In the middle of working a crime scene they had found two things they had in common. They had both spent long stretches of time undercover and they shared a deep love and respect for horses.

"Hey David, you want to come look at this," Sheriff Selter asked two hours into the process.

"What do you have?" he responded.

"I don't know. It looks like a small amount of blood spatter to me," came her answer.

"That's funny, I wonder how it got out here if the horse was in there. I found a little blood in the shavings this morning but I have yet to find its source. Well, like they say in the movies, bag it and tag it," he told her.

"Now who has been watching too much TV?" she joked, remembering his earlier comment.

Following a half a day of backbreaking work, they finally had the barn processed. Lowe spied a travel trailer behind the barn when he was caring evidence bags out to the black-and-white Captain McDowell had dispatched.

"I wonder who lives there? They might have seen or heard something last night," Lowe said to the Sheriff.

A young Mexican man was bringing in some horses from the hot walker. "Why don't you ask him?" Selter suggested.

Lowe called the man over and in perfect Spanish asked about the travel trailer. The man lifted his ball cap above his eyes before he began to speak.

"So the Mise kid lives in the trailer," the Sheriff stated after overhearing the conversation.

"Say, your Spanish is pretty good," Lowe said, complimenting her.

"Just a few years undercover down on the border and I picked a few things up," Selter explained.

"I can't impress you, can I?" he joked.

"Well we're here, it's here. Let's go check it out. The warrant covers the whole ranch and I really don't want to come back and do it tomorrow," she said with a tired look.

"I'm game," was his short answer.

The door to the travel trailer was locked. Lowe was about to suggest that he could go up to the main house and see about getting a key when the Sheriff pulled a small case from her pocket. In no time at all, she had the lock picked and the door open.

"Now I am the one who is impressed. I guess you picked that up as well from your time on the border," Lowe mused.

"The things a girl learns in the service of her country," she said with a laugh.

They didn't know exactly what they were looking for but it didn't take but a minute to find it. On the kitchen table laid the instrument used in the death of Double Ds Delight: a four-foot-long electrical cord with the wires being bared on one end.

"It's looking more and more like the kid did it," Lowe said holding the cord in his hand.

"I still ain't buying it; this is all too easy," she exclaimed, ticking off her reasons for doubt. "Look, all of Mise's belongings are still here. The only thing missing is the kid and his truck. You can't tell me that he got fired, killed the horse and then left without taking so much as his toothbrush. It doesn't add up,"

"This is strange," Lowe said out loud.

"What is strange?" the Sheriff asked

"This window over the table, it's wide open. It doesn't make a lick of sense. The door is locked but the window, without a screen mind you, is wide open," he repeated.

"It makes sense to me, David. The door is locked and you need to do something with the murder weapon. Why not throw it in the window. You take suspicion off of you and put it on Mise," she said, reconstructing her theory of the crime.

"Anyone ever tell you, you have a devious mind, but I like it. We have to find that kid," Lowe said.

It didn't take long to process the small trailer. Lowe dusted for prints on the window but it was clean. Sheriff Selter searched for other evidence pertaining to the crime and found none. The travel trailer was awash, all but the electrical cord and a few unproven theories.

The time had come to make the trip up to the main house and interview Mrs. Brown. The day had been long, and the two just wanted to get it over with. They decided that they would let the lady of the house think that they were half way in agreement with her on the fact that Mise killed the horse.

"Who knows she might slip up and say something we can use," said Lowe, explaining his thinking.

However, it turned out to be wishful thinking. Mrs. Brown would only answer the questions concerning Mise. She described the truck he was driving and what he was wearing the last time she saw him.

She consented to have Sheriff Selter photograph her breast as long as it would be used to bring the lad to justice. Any other questions they may have would have to go through her lawyer. The interview lasted no more than a half hour.

"Our first date was all right, but the second lacked romance," the Sheriff said jokingly, as Lowe walked her to her car.

Lowe couldn't help but laugh. "I'll make it up to you next time, Marcia," he promised.

"You're damn right you will," she said as she drove away leaving him smiling.

CHAPTER 5

THE TAPE

Lowe had just kicked back in his motel room to watch the news. It had been a long day of collecting evidence after the demise of Double Ds Delight. It was; however, the best day he ever had doing the job. Sheriff Marcia Selter saw to that.

He had never met a woman like her. She was pretty, smart, funny and a cop. He had dated before, but none of the women ever understood the job. Selter got it. She knew what it was like because she was living it herself.

He tried to watch the news but his thoughts kept going back to the beautiful woman he had spent the day with. Lowe could tell that she was interested just as much as he was because of the playful jabs back and forth and the flirtation between them.

"Hell, a blind man could see it," he told himself.

He knew he needed to stay focused on the case; it was not the time or place to allow his emotions to run wild with him.

"Why the hell not?" he countered inside his head. She wasn't a suspect; the only thing she was guilty of was trying to steal his heart. Hell he would have gladly given it to her.

Just then a knock came at the door, saving Lowe from his emotional longing. His first thought was that maybe it was the Sheriff, but that was a bit much to hope for. Instead of the beautiful face of Marcia Selter, he found the scraggly mug of Shawn Kelly on the other side of the door.

"I thought you wanted to grab a burger but you look like you're ready to call it a day," Kelly observed.

"I'm sorry Shawn, I forgot all about that. It's been one of those days. Let me grab a clean shirt and we'll go get a bite to eat," Lowe told his friend.

The presence of Kelly afforded Lowe a way to get his mind off of the Sheriff and back on the business at hand. He had questions for his old friend and knowing Kelly as well as he did, he was sure he had questions for him.

"How well do you know Garret Mise?" was Lowe's first question.

"He's been on the ranch ever since he graduated from high school back in May," said Kelly, beginning to fill in the blanks on the only suspect they had at the time. "He's from Arkansas and I've known his folks for years. I roped a little with his daddy,"

"When was the last time you saw the boy?" was Lowe's next question.

"I don't know, maybe six or six-thirty last night. I figured you didn't want him under foot and you ran him off like you did me so you could get your investigating work done. Why?" Kelly asked while taking a bite out of his burger.

"Did he seem shaken or upset when you saw him?" Lowe followed up.

"No Damn it, tell me why you are asking all these question about Garret," Kelly demanded.

"Well Shawn, everybody's pointing the finger at the kid and no one has seen him since last night. I put out an APB (all-points bulletin) on his truck, but it's a very common truck. It's like finding a needle in a haystack," he told Kelly.

"Pointing their finger at him for what?" Kelly asked, getting visibly upset. "Are you telling me they say Garret killed their freaking horse?"

"Calm down," Lowe said, after seeing the man's blood pressure rise. "That's what they're saying, but it doesn't mean I'm buying it."

"What was the reason they gave?" Kelly asked, lowering his voice so the people in the burger joint would stop looking at him.

"Mrs. Brown said he tried to kiss her and then he felt her up. She went as far as pulling her boob out and showing me the bruise. She said she fired him and he threatened to get even," Lowe said, explaining to Kelly what was said.

"That lying bitch!" explained Kelly. "The boy would no sooner hurt that horse, or any horse, than you or I would. If you knew Garret, you would know he has a kind heart; some times a little too kind. It was hard for him to even correct a horse. I have to get on to him every now and then when I see one pushing him.

"Do you know that he is the lowest-paid hand we have on the payroll? Hell, the wets make more than he does. He would work there for free; that's how much the boy loves horses.

"As far as him coming on to the Lilly White Lady of the Manor, that's bullshit too. I don't know how many times he'd come by the house almost in tears because she would try to start kissing on him. He was so afraid he was going to lose his job over her seductions. The woman is a piece of work," Kelly said as his rage bubbled over.

"There's a bit of more bad news," said Lowe. "The horse was electrocuted and the device used was found on the kid's kitchen table. I'm gonna be honest with you Shawn; until I find some motive why the horse was killed, it's not looking too good for Mise. I need to find the boy."

"Didn't you tell me you had it on tape that someone was trying to hire the deed done? Who the hell was on the freaking tape," Kelly wanted to know.

It was a good question, one that Lowe had failed to ask himself. The question would haunt him for the rest of the evening.

"I don't know. I've never heard the recording. We have been going off of what the Feds told us," Lowe confessed.

"Well, don't you think it would be a good idea to listen to the damn thing before putting the noose around the boy's neck," Kelly asked angrily.

"Shawn I don't need you to get mad; I need you to get focused. If you say he didn't do it, he didn't do it, but help me prove it. Do you know where Mise might have gone?" Lowe asked, trying to obtain his friend's help.

Kelly took a deep breath to try to regain his composure before answering. "The only place I can think of is maybe he went home," Kelly said after giving it some thought.

"You mean back to Arkansas?" Lowe asked for clarification.

"Yes! I have his parent's phone number at the house. I'll call them when I get home. I just hate to worry them. His father has a bad ticker. I will call you as soon as I have talked to them," Kelly offered.

"Shawn, don't worry. It will work itself out," Lowe said, trying to reassure his friend.

The two men didn't talk much after that. They just finished the meal and Kelly took Lowe back to his room.

By then, Lowe was feeling guilty, guilty that he had dragged his friend into the mess. He kept racking his brain trying to figure out what he could have done differently but nothing came to mind.

The phone call from Kelly came right before the ten o'clock news.

"David, I talked to Garret's folks. They haven't heard from him since Sunday night. They said he calls every Sunday to check on his daddy. I don't mind telling you, I'm getting worried," Kelly confessed.

"I am sure he'll turn up," Lowe said in a comforting voice. "Like I said, I have an APB out on him. I'll call the Arkansas State Patrol in the morning and see if they can find him. Try to get some sleep and I'll let you know if I hear anything,"

The next morning Lowe put in a call to the local DPS office. He wanted to see if the APB he had put out had yielded anything. The answer was negative. They had yet to find the young, and evidently elusive, Garret Mise.

He then did as he promised Kelly the night before and called the Arkansas State Police. The officer that he spoke to was friendly and assured him that the bulletin would go on the radio waves right away.

He also called the Oklahoma equivalent and asked if they would keep a watchful eye out for Mise. Whitesboro was only a hop, skip and a jump from the Oklahoma border. The kid could be holed up in a motel just across the state line and they would never know it. He knew that he should've done it the day before but with all that was happening, it didn't cross his mind.

Lowe saved the best phone call for last. It was to the lovely Sheriff Marcia Selter. He would be lying to himself if he said he wasn't looking forward to hearing her voice. It was all he had thought about since his eyes opened that morning.

"And a very good morning to you, Officer Lowe," were the words she greeted him with.

"I was thinking Marcia, maybe we ought to take Mrs. Brown up on her offer and invite her and her lawyer in for a sit down," he explained.

"You think we might rattle her into giving up something?" the Sheriff asked.

"Who knows, but I have a few tricks up my sleeve," Lowe confided.

"I am sure you do; it's worth a shot. I'll set it up and get back to you with a time," Selter said.

The meeting was set for after the lunch hour. Selter invited Lowe to come early. She said that she would split half of her tuna sandwich with him and they could talk strategy. The smitten peace officer jumped at the chance.

"I had a thought last night and I almost called you but thought I'd let you rest. Because of the day we put in yesterday, I figured we both could use it," she told him halfway through her sandwich.

"What was that?" Lowe asked.

"You said the Feds heard about this scheme on a wiretap. They had it on tape that someone was trying to hire a hit, if you will, on the horse," she began.

He could not help but recall the conversation the night before that he had with Kelly about the tape.

"Here we go again, back to the damn tape," Lowe thought to himself.

But she surprised him and took it a totally different direction.

88

"What if they hired the kid to kill the stud after the Feds scared the first guy off," she said, putting forth an alternate theory of the crime.

"It's possible but I have it on pretty good authority that Mise didn't have it in him. The story is that he loves horses more than anything," Lowe said, telling her what he had been told by Kelly without using his friend's name.

"You know, as well as I do David, what kind of appeal easy money has on someone. The kid probably never had just a whole lot in his life," the Sheriff pointed out.

"I hear what you're saying, but the kid is barely eighteen, I doubt if he's that jaded yet," Lowe countered. "But then again, all things are possible when cash in on the table," he added.

"Do you have a working theory?" Selter wanted to know.

"It's still a work in progress. I haven't a clue who did the horse in but I am positive that money was involved, one way or another," explained Lowe. "I ain't a found believer in coincidence, not in the world of greed. You can't be overheard trying to hire someone to kill your horse and then claim he was killed because somebody got pissed at you for firing him. It does not wash."

"What about using the angle of hiring the kid to shake the lady?" the Sheriff reasoned out loud.

"That might work if we add in the fact that we have it on tape someone from the Double D was trying to contract the job out," he said, slightly modifying her idea.

I like the way you think, Officer Lowe," Selter mused.

"First, I would like to thank you and your client for coming down, Gary," the Sheriff said, greeting Mrs. Brown and her attorney.

"We only have a few questions, it shouldn't take long," Lowe chimed in.

"I don't know what questions you might have; it seems pretty clear cut to me," Mrs. Brown snipped. "My horse is dead and my stable boy has disappeared. My Lord, it can't be that hard to figure out. It's like one plus one."

"Simmer down JJ, I'll handle this," her lawyer, the honorable Gary W. Thigpin, said.

"It is true that we have a dead horse and the whereabouts of Mr. Mise is unknown but we have just a little more than that," explained Lowe. "It was not by mistake that I was in the area when the horse in question died. I have been working this case for a couple of weeks,"

The fact didn't seemed to faze Mrs. Brown; she just looked away. However, it did peak Thigpin's curiosity.

"What case?" the lawyer wanted to know.

"We have someone from the Double D Ranch on a legal wiretap soliciting a known fugitive to kill the horse. We have the wire, a dead horse and an owner contacting the people who insured the animal not an hour after he was found. You know - one plus one,"

Lowe said, throwing the woman's words back at her.

"We were thinking that your client hired Garret Mise to kill the horse and for all we know he is sipping a fruit drink on some Mexican beach," Sheriff Selter said, taking up her scripted part in the interrogation.

"Well, let's hear the tape," Thigpin demanded.

"Right now the government has it in their custody," Lowe informed the attorney.

"All right Officer Lowe. Is it my client's voice on the tape?" was Thigpin's next question.

"I can't say," Lowe answered.

"Well then, can you say if it's a man's voice or a woman's voice on your precious tape? Have you even heard the thing or are you just some government flunky sent down here to throw around false accusations?" asked the irate lawyer.

"No, we don't have the tape," is all Lowe could say out loud, but inside he was cussing the tape and himself for the interview blowing up in his face.

"Come on JJ, let's go," Thigpin said before storming out of the Sheriff's office. "Call us when you have something or if you find Mise. My client will be pressing charges for the wrongful death of her horse."

"I think that went pretty well," Selter committed.

Lowe couldn't help but laugh but there was something in the way she said it that made him feel a little better.

Lowe apologized to the Sheriff for blowing the interview before leaving her office. He had made a fool out of both of them because he had underestimated the reaction of their opponent. He had also made a fool out of himself with the woman he was growing to like more and more.

"Don't worry about it David," she said consoling him. "We can only play the cards we are dealt. We were playing a bluff and it backfired. It's happened to me more than once and it will happen to both of us again. It was only the first hand; there's a lot more cards to be dealt before this game is over."

That's what was so appealing about the Sheriff; she always saw the bright side. The one thing Lowe did know for a fact was that as soon as he got back to his room, he was gonna call the Captain and ask about the tape. It had bit him on the ass twice; it wasn't going to do it again.

Lowe saw Kelly's truck parked outside his room when he arrived. He looked for the horse trainer but he was nowhere in sight. Across the highway was a coffee shop so he figured Kelly had gone for a cup while waiting for Lowe's return. He put his papers back in his car and started toward the cafe.

He was halfway across the parking lot when he heard his named being called from behind him. He turned to find Kelly coming out of his room.

"I hope you don't mind David. I had the maid let me in. Her cousin used to work for me," Kelly explained.

"Why should I care; we shared a bedroom for seven years," Lowe answered back. "You ain't got a woman in there, do you?" he joked, remembering that had happened a time or two in the past.

"Nope, no one but me. I ain't as young as I used to be. I just got tired of waiting in the truck," the man confessed.

"What's up?" Lowe asked as soon as he entered the room.

"I heard you had a meeting with Brown and her lawyer. I just wondered if they said anything about Garret, or if you heard anything about the boy. His folks have already called me twice today," Kelly said with a worried look.

"I called in this morning and no one has seen hide nor hair of the boy. I have even widened the APB to include Oklahoma. They'll call me when they find him," he assured his old friend.

"I was worried about him last night, now I am really worried. Just between you and me, either I don't know the boy at all and he is in on this, or I do know him as well as I think and he's.....," Kelly's voice tapered off as he was not able to say the unthinkable.

"You're letting your mind play tricks on you, it's not even been two days yet," Lowe said trying to ease Kelly's concerns. "Hell, I can remember when you used to disappear a whole lot longer than that."

"But David, Garret is not me. I know I was as wild as a peach orchard rat but the boy is not like that," Kelly explained.

"My, my, Peter Pan did grow up. Somewhere in heaven Jonah Lowe is dancing a jig. I'll tell you what, let's give it a few more days and if he hasn't turned up, I'll see what else can be done to find your boy. You can give his parents my number if you want," Lowe offered.

Lowe didn't let his friend see it but he was a little worried himself. He was beginning to wonder if his little fraud case wasn't something more. Shit just wasn't adding up. He had to ask himself if Kelly's over concern wasn't wearing off on him and he might be jumping the gun.

The men talked awhile longer before Kelly realized he had things to do back at the ranch. He had a horse in a sale the following day and since Mise was missing, he'd have to get the horse ready by himself. Lowe told Kelly before he left that if he heard anything about the kid, he would call him.

Lowe was alone and he could finally make the call to Captain McDowell. It was something he had wanted to do ever since he had left the Sheriff's office.

"How's the case coming, Lowe?" the Captain asked right off the bat.

"To be perfectly honest Sir, not worth a damn," Lowe answered bluntly.

"How so?" questioned Captain McDowell.

Lowe filled the Captain in on the missing Mise, and how the kid had fallen off the face of the earth - or so it seemed. He told the Captain how all the indicators pointed in the direction of the kid but he felt something wasn't right.

He moved from there to the meeting he and the Sheriff had that afternoon.

"Captain, regarding that wiretap the Feds got, have you heard it? The recording seems to be giving me the most problems. Whoever is on the tape ought to be our number one suspect, but since I haven't heard it, I don't know where to start," he said, unloading his frustration.

"I haven't heard it either but I can see how it might be a stumbling block," said Captain McDowell. "Let me get on the horn with the Feds and see if I can't arrange a sit down.

"Have you heard anything from A&M about our autopsy report? It might be wishful thinking, but it might shed some light," the Captain offered.

"They were going to perform it this afternoon. I thought I might drive down there tomorrow and go over the results in person. All I'm doing up here is getting in my own way until something pops," Lowe explained to his Captain.

"That sounds like a plan," said McDowell. "Call me when you are finished, I'll see if I can set something up with the Feds for the day after tomorrow. You can stop by here and get read-in on your way back to Whitesboro. I don't want you away from the scene too long. Perhaps you can ask the Sheriff to hold the fort down until you get back."

"Roger that Captain, I'll see you in a few days," Lowe said while pushing the button that ended the call on the cellphone.

He felt better after talking to McDowell. At least he might be on the verge of getting somewhere. All he wanted at the moment was a whiskey, a hot shower and some time to idle his brain. He had no whiskey so the other two would have to do.

Lowe was just getting out of the shower when he heard the phone ring. "Lowe," is how he answered it.

"David, it's Marcia. I 'm calling to tell you that I finally found the report on the first Mrs. Brown's suicide. It's not much of a report but knowing my predecessor, I didn't think it would be.

"I tell you what, I could throw some steaks on the grill if you would like to come over and go over it," the Sheriff said while issuing an invite.

Perhaps the day wasn't a total loss. At any rate things were looking up for the Texas peace officer.

"That sounds good to me," he said almost jumping for joy.

"Give me some time to get my critters fed; say about sevenish," Selter said, setting the time.

"I'll see you then," he said hanging up the phone.

Lowe was so excited about getting the invitation to supper that he had forgotten to ask the Sheriff directions to her place. It proved a tad embarrassing having to call her back to find out where she lived.

She laughed, "Some detective you are," she teased before giving him the directions.

Two hours later, Lowe was pulling into the Sheriff's driveway with a bottle of white wine in tow.

Lowe found her watering some flowers in front of her small but quaint ranch house. It was the first time he had ever seen her in anything but her uniform. Her hourglass hips in a tight pair of Wranglers were nothing short of jaw dropping. He had to keep reminding himself that he was there to go over a report with her.

"I see you found the place. The report is in the house on the bar. Why don't you go look over it while I finish my watering," she suggested.

Lowe agreed. However, what he really wanted to do was stay and look at her. But that would have been way too obvious.

He found the report lying on the bar labeled "Jane Brown." His investigative skills kicked in right away. John and Jane Brown. That sounded too close to John and Jane Doe but at the moment, it was just a curiosity. Lowe opened the file and began to study the contents.

"Not a whole lot in there, is there?" she asked entering the house some ten minutes later.

"I don't know, there's a few things that peak my interest," he said holding up a picture of the late Mrs. Brown's body.

"Such as?" the Sheriff wanted to know.

"For starters, you can tell by the pictures that Mrs. Brown was a very attractive woman. Statistics say that it's uncommon for women to use a gun to kill themselves. Overdose, more times than not, is the method used. Beautiful women usually don't shoot themselves in the head when they do use a firearm. It's something in the female psyche that tells them they have to be presentable even in death," said Lowe, quoting from a paper he had read.

"I see what you are saying. A woman, especially from her class, has been taught almost from birth that appearances matter above all else," said the Sheriff, rewording what Lowe had just said.

"Now look at the wound itself. Do you see any speckling or muzzle burns?" Lowe pointed out. "A close-contact wound like that should have both. I just wonder if there was GSR (gun shot residue) on her hands or clothing."

"It doesn't say anything about it in the report because I had the same questions," Selter said. "I don't know if that page was lost or even if it was included at all."

"Surely it was; it's standard operating procedure," Lowe said in a dumbfound tone.

"David, you don't know how relaxed things were around here before I took over. It took me half of my first term just to get the case files in order. What seems standard to you or me was none existent to the last administration," Selter explained to Lowe.

"Look at the wound Marcia, it is on the left side of her head. It would be acceptable if she was left-handed, but what if she wasn't?" Lowe said, leaving the obvious left hanging.

"Perhaps she was left-handed," said Selter. "It ought to be fairly easy to find out. All we have to do is find someone who knew her and ask them."

"I know just the person who would know for sure," said Lowe thoughtfully. "Her horse trainer, Shawn Kelly. I'll ask him; we go way back."

"I know Shawn, I didn't realized you did. How far back do you go with him?" she said in a surprised tone.

"About as far as two people can go. He worked for my grandfather after his mother died," he explained.

"You are just full of surprises; a regular man of mystery," Selter said smiling at him.

"The GSR report is not the only thing missing. Where is the medical examiner's report?" Lowe asked after going through the file a few times.

"Knowing how lazy my predecessor was, he probably never went to Denton and picked it up. I bet it is still sitting down there," said Selter, making a guess.

"I have to go to College Station tomorrow for the autopsy report on Double Ds Delight. I guess I can stop in Denton and see if they have the report on the death of the first Mrs. Brown," Lowe told the Sheriff.

"How long are you going to be gone," she asked with a bit of sadness.

"Not long, a few days,' he relayed to Selter. "The Captain wants me to stop at headquarters for a meeting with the Feds about everybody's favorite wiretap. We actually may get to hear the thing. I am hoping it will shed some light on the case. He asked me to see if you'll mind the store while I'm gone."

"You know I will, David," she said as she offered him a drink. "Now enough shop talk; if I don't put those steaks on, it's gonna be midnight before supper is ready."

Lowe followed his hostess out to the grill with his drink in hand. He could tell by watching her how she was so quick to get the warrant on the Double D Ranch. The view from his vantage point was simply amazing; so much so that she had to ask him twice how he liked his steak cooked.

However, the fact that was absent to him was that she was checking him out when his back was turned. The attraction was so thick you could have made pancakes out of it, yet each was hesitant to make the first move.

"Would you watch the meat while I go inside and make the salad," she asked of her guest.

"I think I can handle that," Lowe replied.

Thinking to herself as she sliced and diced the vegetables, she realized that if a move was to be made that night, it was apparent she would have to make it.

"He might be a good criminal detective but he's lacking in the detection of the signs of romance," she mused.

Lowe was about to turn the steaks over when he felt her hand caress the small of his back. He became weak in the knees when she pressed her body next to his. The temptation was so great that he fought it no more. He turned and watched as her lips rose to meet his.

Their first kiss was long and deep, the kind that he felt in his loins. It was a kiss that he would not soon forget and the next one was just as pleasurable. The case seemed to disappear into a distant memory as the passion of the moment rushed over both of them.

"I heard that cold steak tastes just as good," Lowe said, whispering in her ear.

"I do have a microwave," she whispered back before leading him into the house.

Night had long since fallen when they emerged back to the place where their first kiss had taken place hours earlier. They ate like two bears who had just awakened from a long sleep, with each one being too tired to speak. A glow fell over the patio as they exchanged one smile after another.

The silence of the night was broken by yelps coming from her barn.

"I forgot about the pups, I guess I best go check on them," she said, rising to her feet.

"What pups?" he asked after hearing about them for the first time.

"My collie, Toy, has a litter. She's been trying to wean them for a few days. Her little ones are not giving up the tit without a fight," the Sheriff explained.

"You mind if I go with you? I'll give them the once over; after all, I am a certified veterinarian," Lowe boasted humorlessly.

"So people keep telling me," she kidded with her newly mined lover. "I knew if I let you hang around long enough, I could find other uses for you."

The noise coming from the barn became louder as they approached. It was like the puppies could hear their cries being answered. She opened the door and one of the pups raced out to greet her.

"Did you think I forgot about you," Selter spoke in a loving tone as she picked up the pup.

Two others ran to her when she turned the light in the barn on. Lowe could see the momma dog sitting up on a bale of hay. He reasoned it was so high that she knew her bothersome brood would not try to nurse.

He was about to pick up one of the little canine fur balls to examine it when out of the shadows a fourth one appeared. The pup looked nothing like the rest of his littermates.

The pup was red with big green eyes and he was also larger than the rest. But the most striking attribute about him was the size and shape of his head. It was big and square. He was simply the ugliest dog Lowe had ever seen.

Selter could tell he was trying to put the pieces of the puzzle together. "I paid good money to have Toy bred. A day before she went out of season, the mutt next door paid us a visit. That little guy is the end result," she explained.

"Come here, you little meathead," Lowe called out to the pup.

The dog stopped and changed his course as soon as he heard Lowe's voice. He ran straight to him and sat on the toe of his boot.

"You're so damn ugly you're cute," Lowe said as he picked the pup up and held him in his arms.

"That answers that question," Selter replied as she saw the pup snuggle close to the man's chest.

"What question would that be?" Lowe asked as he stroked the dog's red fur.

"The other puppies are all spoken for. I was wondering what I was going to do with "Little Meathead," as you called him," she answered.

"Wait a minute, I see where this is going," Lowe protested.

"You two were meant to be together," Selter said laughing.

"Marcia, I am always on the road. I ain't been home for nearly three weeks as it is. What am I going to do with him?" he asked in protest.

"Have you ever read any of the Jesse Stone crime novels?" Selter asked. "Jesse always had his trusty dog with him."

"If I remember right, Stone was a drunk," Lowe fired back.

"But he always had his dog," she pointed out.

He knew then, he would never be able to resist her. It was no use even trying.

"All right Meathead; it looks like we are stuck with each other," Lowe whispered to the pup.

Lowe left Sheriff Selter's house that night with more than he came with: an ugly mutt of a dog and, if he was lucky, a beautiful woman's heart.

CHAPTER 6

NEED TO KNOW

It had to be a dream. Maybe if he rolled over, the horrible noise would go away. Lowe tried and yet the pounding persisted. The night before had been heavenly being held in Marcia Selter's arms. Perhaps the constant pounding, that a pillow over his head wouldn't stop, was a way to punish him.

"Damn it David, are you in there?" It was no dream, just Shawn Kelly beating on the door to his room.

It took him back two decades and how his old friend used to wake him up for school.

"Damn it boy, get up. One of us needs an education and it ain't gonna be me," Kelly would say.

"Alright, alright, give me a minute," Lowe yelled as he was getting out of bed.

He grabbed his jeans, put them on, and stumbled his way to the door. He nearly stepped on the little red ball of fur curled up beside the bed. In his slumber, he had forgotten about his new dog.

"Long night?" Kelly asked when Lowe finally opened the door.

"My God Shawn, it's six in the morning. It wasn't as long a night as much as you made it a short one," Lowe grumbled.

"Here you old sourpuss; I brought you some coffee," Kelly offered as he pushed his way through the door.

"You're welcome to come in," Lowe said after the fact.

"What the hell! Damn David, that has got to be the ugliest pup I have ever seen," Kelly noted after seeing the dog for the first time.

"Shawn, Meathead. Meathead, Shawn," he said, introducing his new pet that was still half asleep.

It didn't take a mental giant to know why Kelly had dropped by at six in the morning. He had questions and they weren't only about the puppy that was at the moment sitting in his lap. The questions the man had were the same he had the day before and the ones he would have in the days coming, until they found Garret Mise.

The worry was all over Kelly's face, and Lowe saw it. Kelly had always had a way with kids. It was like kids and horses were his specialty. Lowe had even put one in his custody after arresting his dope-selling parents. It had turned out well for the young man who was about to graduate from college in the spring.

"Let me get a shower real quick and then we can talk," Lowe suggested. "It won't do neither one of us any good if I am still half asleep. Why don't you take Meathead for a walk while I wash yesterday off?"

Lowe could hear his old friend talking to the pup when he got out of the shower. It was almost comical how grown men would talk to animals when they thought no one was around.

"Now, what can I do you for, Shawn?" Lowe asked as soon as he was finished with his morning grooming.

"I was wondering if there had been any word about the boy?" Kelly asked, just as Lowe had predicted.

"Not as of last night. I'll call this morning before I leave," he told his friend.

"Leave? Where the hell are you going?" Kelly questioned, getting rather excited.

"I have to make a run down to College Station," said Lowe. "They ought to have the autopsy report done on the horse. I have a meeting tomorrow in Austin, then I'll be back tomorrow night sometime.

"Don't worry Shawn, I am coming back. You will be the first one I will notify if I hear anything about Mise," Lowe assured his friend.

Lowe's words seemed to calm the old horse trainer down for the moment. He knew it was only temporary. He also knew as sure as he was sitting there, that the first call he would get the next morning would be from Kelly.

He had to get his friend's focus somewhere else before he worried himself sick.

Lowe then had an idea; one that he felt would kill two birds with one stone.

"Hey Shawn old buddy, would you do me a favor while I am gone," he asked in a way that made Kelly know something was up.

"Oh no, not me," said Shawn. "I know where this is headed. You want me to dog-sit this ugly mutt. I got horses to see after, you know?" he tried to explain but he knew there was no getting out of the chore."

"Don't worry, it's only for a few days," Lowe said in a convincing voice after he knew his friend would say yes.

"Where in the hell did you get thing ugly thing at anyway?" Kelly asked.

"Marcia conned me into taking the little guy last night," was his answer.

"About the same way you just conned me into dog sitting," Kelly concluded.

"Not exactly," Lowe said smiling ear to ear.

"You old dog. I guess I did teach you a thing or two," Kelly said with a smile after he put two and two together.

"I almost forgot Shawn," Lowe said after remembering the police report of the suicide from the night before. "Do you know if the late Jane Brown was right or left handed?"

"Right handed. Why?" Kelly answered.

"Just something I am following up on," Lowe said, holding back his suspicions.

Lowe was on the road headed south an hour later. His first stop was in Denton, Texas, to have a conversation with the medical examiner.

The answer he had received from Kelly that morning had spiked his interest. It would be hard for the woman to shoot herself in the left side of her head if she was right handed. Hard, but not impossible! That is why he wanted to talk with the examiner.

He began to question his own ideas halfway to Denton. Could it be that he was looking for something that wasn't there. He had yet to come up with a reasonable theory about the case at hand, perhaps he was grasping at straws. He had been sent to investigate a fraud case, not a ten-year-old suicide. Something still seemed fishy and he could not overlook it.

Dr. Mark Vohn was the medical examiner for Denton County as well as the smaller counties that surrounded it. Lowe knew that because he had made an appointment with Vohn before leaving Gainesville.

Dr. Vohn was waiting in his office when Lowe arrived. He rose from his desk, shook the DPS officer's hand and returned to the sitting position.

"What case are you working on Officer Lowe?" was the doctor's first question.

"It's one of your old suicide cases. It's not really the case I am working on but they may be related," Lowe explained.

"Alright what was the last name?" was the next question that Vohn asked.

"Brown," came Lowe's one-word answer.

"Jane Brown," the doctor said as the color drained from his face.

"Yes sir, do you remember the case?" Lowe asked. But no answer was necessary. He could tell by the look on the doctor's face that he remembered the case.

"I just knew some day that case would come back to bite me in the ass," said the doctor. "It was a real cluster, you know what, from the get go.

"The idiot sheriff sent the body to the mortuary before I caught wind of it. Any damn fool knows any suspicious death has to come to the Medical Examiner's Office first. I had the body brought here after reading about it in the newspaper.

"By the time I had her on my table, it was too late for any trace evidence to be collected. The body had been washed and what it could have told us, went down the drain," Dr. Vohn recalled.

"So there was no gun shot residue or speckling?" Lowe inquired.

"Not a speck. Like I said, the body had been cleaned," the doctor repeated.

"What about a muzzle burn?" Lowe questioned.

"Nope, and I thought that was more than just a little strange," Vohn committed.

"Did you know that the victim was right handed?" said Lowe, questioning the medical examiner. "I asked that because I looked at some photos of the body and the wound was on the left side of the head,"

"The paper work I received said she was left-handed," explained Vohn. "You think that is strange Officer Lowe? Let me tell you, that's the half of it. I cut the body open and it was not surprising that a bullet to the brainpan killed her; it usually will.

"Suicide isn't always as cut and dried as it may seem. A whole host of factors can come into play, the least of which is foul play. Questions have to be answered, such as, 'Was she drunk or under the influence of any drugs.' Both could explain the use of the left hand. For example: if she was drinking, her right hand could have been holding a glass or bottle.

"I followed procedures and ordered up blood and tissue work as well as a toxicology screen. You know as well as I do how long lab reports take; it's not like it's do or die. Pardon the M.E. humor.

"Three weeks later the reports came back and as soon as I sat down to read them, the FBI shows up and takes them. It was the damndest thing I ever saw. They said it pertained to an on-going investigation.

"I just knew that someday somebody would come asking questions and here you are," Vohn said finishing his story.

Lowe was speechless. He was a little suspicious before talking to Vohn, but after hearing the man's story, he was a long way past that. He knew there had to be a logical explanation but for the life of him, he couldn't come up with one. The good news was that he and the Captain were meeting with the Feds the next day. Perhaps they could shed some light on the mystery.

He thanked Dr. Vohn for his time and was on his way again.

An hour later, the conversation with the medical examiner was still on his mind. He was just south of Fort Worth when his cellphone rang. His first thought was that it was probably Kelly all worked up again, or perhaps Meathead had eaten something he wasn't supposed to: like Kelly's best pair of boots. The thought made him laugh out loud.

Lowe was pleasantly surprised when he heard, "Hey handsome, how's my favorite dinner date?" the beautiful Sheriff was asking as only she could.

"Favorite, you mean there's more," he said playfully.

"I'll never tell," Selter told him. "By the way, how is Officer Meathead this morning?" she asked after a slight pause.

"I left him with Shawn; he needed something other than Garret Mise to worry over for a spell," said Lowe, explaining the whereabouts of the pup. "I fear this whole deal with the kid is getting to him."

She then wanted to know if Lowe had asked Kelly if the late Mrs. Brown was right or left handed. He gave the answer he was told: "right" and then went on to tell her the strange story he had heard from Dr. Vohn.

"Sometimes you have to wonder if the crazies are right. Could it be just one big conspiracy theory," she asked after hearing the tale.

"I don't know, but something stinks to high heaven," Lowe committed.

They discussed the strangeness of the case awhile longer before moving on to a much more enjoyable topic, mainly the love they had made the night before. The conversation was so deep that before Lowe knew it, he was almost to San Antonio.

"Marcia I'm gonna have to get off at this exit and get some gas. I'll call you tonight when I get done with my meeting at A&M," he said pulling off of I-35. He did; however, thank her for making his day before hanging up.

Lowe found Dr. Jackie Bingham, the Dean of the School of Veterinarian Medicine waiting for him after he picked up his visitor's parking pass. Lowe had known the man for over twenty years. He was one of Lowe's professors long before Bingham was the Dean of the college.

"Damn good to see you David, it has been too long," he said to Lowe.

Lowe returned the gesture and they shook hands.

"Your report is finished David; I have it on my desk. You said it was important so I did the autopsy myself.

"You called the death correctly. It was by electrocution." Bingham declared.

"Hell Doc, a blind man could have made that call. I am more concerned with the horse's reproductive system," Lowe said to his one-time professor.

"Let me start by saying, a hundred-and-ten volts of electricity running through a body, any body, causes serious damage," Bingham reported. "That said, I was able to run a few tests on the horse's sperm count. I concluded from the test that the count was weak and in rapid decline. The stud would've been, for all purposes, a gelding within six months. But that is the good news."

"And the bad news, Doc?" Lowe asked.

"Well David, I don't know if you could prove my findings in a court of law. The utter destruction caused by the current racing through the horse calls most tests into question," Bingham pointed out.

"I was afraid of that Doc, but is there enough there for a bluff," was Lowe's next question.

"I would say so, especially with my report. Come on in the office and I'll get it for you," Bingham said holding the door open for him.

Lowe sat in Bingham's office skimming over the autopsy report. He would raise his eyes and look at his old teacher and ask him a question every now and then. He felt it was a good use of his time as he didn't want to get down the road and then have a question. But it was not all business because he enjoyed seeing Bingham.

Dr. Bingham liked the times he got to see his old pupil and they would sometimes talk for hours. The professor would often quiz Lowe about his cases. The professor was always intrigued about the young man's career choice as it wasn't the normal path for one of his students, and he knew Lowe was making a difference by working with the Department of Public Safety.

Lowe indulged the man with the details of his latest case after he finished reading the autopsy report. It seemed like the least he could do after what the Dean had done for him. Bingham listened to his story as Lowe took him through all of the twists and turns of the case.

"Who was the attending vet?" Bingham asked after Lowe finished telling him about the case. "A horse worth that kind of money has a vet on call 24-7."

"Dr. Jason Southerland. Why?" Lowe wanted to know.

" The reason why I asked who the horse's vet was because he had to know his semen was deteriorating. In fact, if the horse was killed because of his future sterilization, his vet would have to have known about his condition. Who else would tell the owners, putting this whole plot in motion," Bingham stated.

"That's a good point; one that needs a closer look," Lowe said after considering what the college dean had said. "Doc, if you ever get tired of teaching, I'll get you a job with the department."

"Who's this Dr. Southerland?" Bingham wanted to know.

"He strikes me as a bit prickly," confided Lowe, "but I was only around him that first day and I haven't seen the man since."

"That ought to tell you something, David," Bingham told his former student. "If it was an animal under my care, I'd want to know what happened. I would be on the phone with you every day, if for no other reason than liability."

Lowe thanked the Dean of the college for his input on the case and for doing the autopsy on the horse. The two discussed a few more unrelated topics before Lowe said it was time for him to go.

It had been a long day and he had covered some miles. He still had to drive home, a place he hadn't seen in three weeks. Home for Lowe was a rented house on the outskirts of Austin. He had planned on moving back to his grandfather's place but the daily drive would have been murder.

He stopped at the mailbox and picked up three weeks of bills and junk mail before entering the house. The sun was just about to disappear into the west when he considered his day done. It was past the time for a drink and perhaps a bite to eat.

Lowe had gone through his mail, ate dinner and was on his second drink by nine. He never knew how lonely his life was up until then. A night spent in the arms of a woman as beautiful as Marcia Selter might have been the reason behind what he was feeling at the moment.

He understood for the first time why his friend Lucius Defoe had so many dogs. The dogs kept the loneliness at bay.

He had a choice: he could have another drink and feel lonely or he could give Selter a call. He opted for the latter.

He felt so much better just hearing the sound of her voice, yet he still longed for the taste of her lips and the warmth of her touch. It was a high that a bottle of whiskey would never give him.

Selters asked him how it had gone in College Station. He told her of his meeting, and all the details.

"What do you know about Dr. Southerland?" he wanted to know.

"You mean Dr. Proctologist, that's what some call him," she told Lowe.

"Why is that?" Lowe asked almost chuckling.

"Cause all his client are ass holes," she said, letting him in on the joke that had been circulating for years.

His chuckle turned into a roar of laughter after hearing the punch line. She was sure enough a pistol. The laugh did the officer a world of good after the long day he had.

"Enough about the case my love. Don't you think it's time we find out what else we have in common besides this case," she asked, trying to push the conversation in another direction.

Due to the fact that she called him "her love," he couldn't help but see her point. They began to talk about horses, as he knew that would make her happy. He too loved horses but it had been years since he had owned one. He always thought that part of him had died with his grandfather but she was bringing that passion back to life.

"Let's go riding the first free chance we get," she said, flirting with Lowe. "I want to see how you look in the saddle Officer Lowe."

"I probably look a little rusty; it's been awhile since I have been a horseback," he said with a laugh. "You might have to cut me a little slack."

The late-night conversation went on for another forty-five minutes before they ran out of things to say. It was nearing midnight when goodbyes were finally exchanged.

Lowe left about seven a.m. the next morning for headquarters. He wanted to get there early so he could go by the crime lab to see if any of the reports were in.

His curiosity surrounded one test in particular: the blood found both inside and outside of the horse's stall. The autopsy report he had read the day before was void of any mention of an open wound on Double Ds Delight's body and he hadn't seen a wound on the day he examined the dead horse. The source of the wound might be critical in the case. But then again it might be nothing.

Lowe knew that Jonita Polk, the lab tech, arrived a little before eight each morning. It was said around headquarters that you could set your watch by the woman's punctual arrival.

"Well hello stranger, I haven't seen you in a few weeks," was how the friendly lab tech greeted him.

"Hi Jonita, the Captain has had me working a case up in North Texas," Lowe told the woman.

"I know, he said you might be in this morning to look at some results," Polk explained. "I say 'some' because I don't have all the tests run yet."

"What about the trace-blood droplets I sent. Do you have anything on those?" Lowe asked.

"I got some but not all the results on the blood yesterday. I can tell you it's human and it is O-positive. However, I can't tell you how old it is," the lab tech explained. "I can send it off but there's no guarantee they'll have any better luck than I did. The technology just isn't there yet, David."

"At least it's something," Lowe said. "What else do you have?" he asked.

Polk went over the findings with him that she did have; however, none were earth shattering. The type of electrical cord used to kill the horse could be found just about anywhere. The trace he and the Sheriff collected was to be expected in any horse barn and so on.

Lowe told her he had to meet with the Captain, then thanked her and asked her to call if she found out anything else.

The next stop for him that morning was Captain McDowell's office. Lowe had no idea what time the federal agents were due to arrive, but he wanted to talk to the Captain before they did. He had reports to go over with him so they would be on the same page when their guest did get there.

He had to talk to McDowell concerning his little visit to the Medical Examiner's Office the day before. Lowe wanted to see if his commanding officer got the same strange vibes off the Brown suicide report or the lack of one. The Captain might have a better idea what was going on. Lowe accepted the fact there were things above his pay-grade.

"Captain do you have any idea why the Feds would interfere with a suicide investigation," Lowe asked when he had McDowell bring him up to speed.

"I have no clue, Lowe. It may all be unrelated or it could be they're using us to keep their hands clean," the Captain let it be known. "God only knows why the Feds do what they do. I almost turned this case down just because of shit like this."

"Why didn't you, sir?" Lowe asked.

"I didn't turn them down because they asked for you. I felt like it was a good way to get you back in the game. After all, it was just a fraud case," said McDowell.

"I don't know Lowe. Hell we may be just getting ahead of ourselves. Perhaps we will have a better understanding once we talk to them. They ought to be here in about thirty minutes. Why don't you go grab a cup off coffee and I'll call you when they show," McDowell suggested.

Lowe was downstairs in the break room working on his second cup of coffee when a young officer came to get him.

"Captain McDowell sent me to find you; he needs you in his office," the man stated.

Lowe was about thirty feet from the Captain's office when he heard McDowell explode. "What do you mean, 'It's need to know?' Damn it, it's my officer in the field and I who need to know," the Captain yelled, going off on the men in his office.

"Sorry I am late," Lowe said entering the doorway. He thought if he interrupted the tense situation, it might give the Captain time to regain his composure.

"I am officer Lowe, the man working the Brown case," he said offering his hand to the two well-dressed agents.

The two men introduced themselves as Special Agents Swink and Diggs of the FBI. The three men shook hands and then turned to face McDowell. The Captain had calmed down a bit since Lowe had interjected himself into the meeting.

"Lowe, they say they have the tape but we are not allowed to hear the thing," the Captain told him.

"Like we were telling the Captain, the tape is part of a very sensitive, on-going investigation," one of the field agents explained.

"I see, could you at least tell us if the voice on the tape belongs to a male or a female?" Lowe said, trying an in-run.

The two FBI agents consulted with one another before answering. "We can tell you it is a man's voice heard on the recording," one of the agents reported.

"Alright, now we are getting somewhere. Captain, did you ask them about that other item we were discussing earlier," Lowe asked.

"Not yet, I was trying to get what I thought was the easy stuff out of the way first," said McDowell biting his tongue.

"The course of my investigation led me to an old suicide: the Jane Brown suicide," said Lowe; however, he had no sooner got the words out of his mouth when one of the agents pounced.

"That has nothing to do whatsoever with your case. Just forget all about the woman's suicide. Perhaps we need to take over the fraud case." the man responded, making it sound like Lowe had touched a nerve.

"Over my dead body," the Captain said, blowing up as he reached for the phone. Do you remember that you're the ones who called us. I have too many man hours involved to quit now."

"It won't do any good to call our supervisor; he will just tell you the same thing," one of the agents pointed out.

"I am not calling your boss, I am calling my cousin, the freaking Attorney General," the Captain said while gritting his teeth.

The two agents seemed to be dumbfounded over McDowell's reaction.

"Sir, there's no need in that. I am sorry; I just spoke too quickly. Go ahead with your fraud case; just tread lightly. Remember, there are other considerations," said the agent while backtracking.

The agents tried to smooth things over before they made their getaway. Lowe was just glad he was in the room to stop it from coming to blows. It had been some time since he had seen someone as mad as his Captain.

"That went well, didn't it Lowe?" stated the Captain after the agents had departed. We don't know anymore than we did."

"I don't know Captain, at least I know it was a man's voice on the tape," he pointed out.

"And that helps, how?" the Captain asked with a tinge of anger still in his tone.

"It narrows the field," said Lowe. "I always thought it was the wife who did the horse in. My assumption was based on the fact that she would be the one who had the most to gain. She was listed as the sole beneficiary on the policy.

"The trainer has nothing to gain; he's only in charge of the horses that are still racing; the management of the stallions and their stud fees are run by somebody else. My guess at the moment would be that it was John Brown, the only one I haven't checked out.

"He was away on business and as far as I know, he is still in Houston, but he could have had someone do it for him. Men like Brown don't like getting their hands dirty," finished Lowe.

"What about the Mise kid? Do you think he had anything to do with it?" McDowell asked.

"Don't know Captain. It's like he has fallen off the planet. I have people looking for him in three states. If he didn't do it, he knows something; that's if he's even still alive. I found blood in the horse's stall and splatter outside the stall. The lab says it's human," he reported.

"You're a good cop, Lowe. If you wouldn't have been here today, I don't know what I would have done. Those federal sons of bitches really had my ass hairs up. Did you see that one start craw fishing when I threatened to call the Attorney General? Them bastards are hiding something," McDowell confided.

"I never knew your cousin was the Attorney General," Lowe said.

"How do you think I saved your job back when you and Defoe got into that mess on the border? Said McDowell with a smile. "Speaking of Defoe, I want you to call him. See if he has anyone on the inside of the Bureau; I want to know what they're not telling us. Defoe has been around so long, he knows all the players," said the Captain.

"Knowing Lucius the way I do, he's pissed half of them off," Lowe said with a laugh.

"That might be so but I bet the other half owes him a favor or two," McDowell guessed.

"You do know Lucius," Lowe chuckled. "I'll get right on it sir. Anything else?" he asked.

Fifteen minutes after leaving the Captain's office, Lowe picked up the phone to call Defoe. He hadn't spoken with the ranger since that day at the coffee shop when he had met that crazy Texan Bubba Lee and his dog. Lowe wondered if the West Texas cowboy ever made it to the islands.

"David, David Lowe is that really you. Son, I was just fixin' to head up a search party and come find your no-calling ass," Defoe said teasing when Lowe got hold of him on the phone.

"I am sorry about that Lucius; I caught a case," Lowe tried to explain.

"Yes I know. I knew it was just a matter of time before McDowell let you off the leash. How does it feel to be back in the saddle?" the ranger asked.

"It beats the hell out of watching the game from the sidelines," he answered.

"I bet it does. Now what can I do for you today?" Defoe wanted to know.

"I am having a time getting a straight answer out of the FBI about this case. As sure as I am sitting here, I know they're hiding something. You don't happen to have someone in the agency who might un-muddy the water, do you?" Lowe questioned.

"Imagine that, the Feds holding something back. It sounds like I can name that tune in two notes. Let me make a few calls and see what I can come with. Is McDowell onboard with this? Do you remember what happened the last time we tried an end around?" Defoe reminded Lowe.

"Believe it or not Lucius, he told me to call you. The Feds really pissed him off," Lowe explained.

He then went over the particulars of the Brown case with the ranger. Defoe told him to give him a few days to make some calls. He would be in touch. Lowe gave the ranger his cell number before saying goodbye. Lowe was back in his car headed north shortly after the call with Defoe ended.

CHAPTER 7

THE KING IS DEAD

Lowe's plan when he left Austin was to pick up Meathead first thing when he got back to Whitesboro. He was sure Kelly would pepper him with questions about the Mise kid so he wanted to get that out of the way. He had checked on the status of his all-points bulletin before leaving Austin; there was still no word on the kid.

Twenty miles from his destination, the urge hit him. Lowe knew Selter would be home by the time he got there and more than anything else, he wanted to see her. He hadn't heard her voice since the night before and he hadn't seen her in two days. He would grow to love the pup but that day the beautiful Sheriff won out.

The look of joy on the Lowe's face turned to one of confusion when he saw Kelly's old truck in the Sheriff's drive.

"I hope I ain't headed for a train wreck," he said to himself as he got out of his car. Who knew what stories his old friend might be telling her about their misguided youth.

Meathead met him at the door, his little tail going ninety to nothing. It was clear to see that the pup had formed a bound with his new owner a bit faster than Lowe.

"Come on in David," Selter said greeting him. "We were just talking about you,"

"Marcia you do realize Shawn is a horse trainer and they are subject to stretching the truth," Lowe warned.

"I see you found my note," Kelly asked.

"No what now? I just now got back," Lowe quickly answered, hoping that he might score a few points if Selter knew he came to see her first. He might need them if Kelly let on that he knew they had been together.

"I brought that dog of yours over here because I have to go to the airport and pick up Kelly Sue," Kelly informed Lowe.

"Alright I'll play, who's Kelly Sue," Lowe asked as he was picking the pup up off the floor so he wouldn't step on him.

"Kelly Sue Brown, the daughter. Remember I told you about her," Kelly said trying to invoke Lowe's memory.

"You said he had a daughter but I don't think you mentioned her name," Lowe replied.

"My bad, I guess with everything going on around here, I left that part out," Kelly explained. "Anyway she's been away at school. Brown called me this morning and asked me to go get her."

"I haven't seen her in a few years," said Lowe. "How old is she now?" the Sheriff asked.

"She'll be twelve in December. She don't care too much for her stepmother and I think it's mutual.

She begged Brown to let her go off to school to avoid the queen bitch," Kelly answered.

The way the horse trainer talked about the girl, it was easy to see he was looking forward to her visit. He was in his Sunday best and was clean-shaven. Kelly then invited the two to come watch her show her horse the following weekend.

"I'm not sure that's a good idea, old buddy. Marcia and I are investigating foul play on the ranch. I don't imagine it would sit too well for us to show up at the girl's horse show. Me and Marcia are the last people they want to see," Lowe said, pointing out the obvious.

"It doesn't matter; they never show up to watch Kelly Sue anyway," said Kelly. "John Brown's idea of parenting is throwing money at the child and JJ is so into herself that she doesn't give a damn. It would be a hell of a lot different if Jane were alive. Why she'd be right there doing my job for me." As Kelly spoke, a touch of sadness invaded the glee he was feeling only a moment earlier.

"That is so sad," Selter committed.

"Let's see how the case goes," Lowe offered. "If I ain't running around like a chicken with my head cut off, I'll be there."

"Could I get you to turn back?" Kelly joked,

"Don't push it, Shawn," Lowe fired back just as playful.

"Don't let him kid you Marcia. There was a time when David was the best horseman in ten counties.

The boy could sure sit a saddle," Kelly bragged on his friend.

"How many decades ago was that, Shawn?" Lowe answered back.

"Speaking of John Brown, and not to change the subject, it seems he moved to the top of our suspect list," Lowe told the other two.

"I don't see it," Kelly said, speaking his mind. "Don't get me wrong, there's not a lot I'd put past him but he's a numbers guy. A million dollar insurance policy is a drop in the bucket to him. Besides all that, the horse was still siring. It just doesn't make sense, not to me."

"According to the horse's autopsy report, the stud's potential was about to play itself out. A stallion shooting blanks has very little value," Lowe reported.

"And that is only the half of it. The Feds wouldn't let us hear the wiretap tape but they did confirm it was a man's voice. I can't think of another man who had as much to gain," Lowe continued, summing it up.

"So now what?" the Sheriff asked.

"Shawn, do you have his office number. I don't want to have another run-in with Lawyer Thigpen if I can help it. I am going to arrange an appointment for an interview with Brown. I want to see how he reacts to the evidence we have thus far," Lowe explained.

"I have his business card; it has his office number," Kelly said while reaching for his wallet.

Lowe had planned on asking Kelly some more questions about the suicide of the late Mrs. Brown, but after seeing the man's sadness earlier, he decided not to. He would just wait and see what Defoe could come up with. He saw no need in bringing up the subject and inflicting more grief. Lowe could tell his old friend had a soft spot for the woman.

"I guess I best be getting to the airport," Kelly said rising from his seat.

"Wait a minute Shawn. I'll walk you to your pick-up," Lowe offered.

"Have you heard anything, David," the man asked when they got outside.

Lowe didn't even have to ask Kelly to clarify the question. He knew the man was asking about the missing boy. "No, not yet," was all Lowe said.

"Do you do know what kind of dog you have there?" Kelly asked referring to the pup trailing behind Lowe. "He is a rare breed for these parts,"

"I can't say that I do," Lowe said, knowing there was a punch line coming sometime in the near future.

"He is an 'Iwanna' dog, like I wanna freaking biscuit," Kelly said joking but trying to hide his emotions about the Mise boy.

"I want to thank you for watching my Iwanna dog while I was gone," Lowe told the man before he drove off.

He turned after waving bye to his friend, only to find the pup digging in Selter's flowerbed.

"You stop that, Meathead. I want a freaking biscuit, my ass. More like I want to get David shot," Lowe said, laughing to himself.

The minute Lowe walked back through the door, Selter wrapped her arms around him and kissed him deeply.

"I've been wanting a kiss like that ever since I left," he committed when she allowed him to come up for air.

"I've been wanting to give you one ever since you left," Selter said with a smile.

"You want to grab a bite to eat?" he asked but she shook her head "no."

"I guess that didn't work out too good last time," Lowe said taking her into his embrace.

Lowe was hard at it the next morning. He wanted to review all the reports he had collected while he was gone. He had to make sure he hadn't overlooked something before making his next move.

The next thing on his agenda was calling to make an appointment with John Brown. He thought it strange after everything that had happened that he hadn't seen the man. He hadn't received so much as a phone call.

Lowe called the number Kelly had given him the night before and that led to another number and so on. It took Lowe half the day to track Brown down. He finally reached the man's personal assistant after having to recharge his cellphone twice.

Brown's assistant assured Lowe that his boss knew nothing about the happenings of the last ten days. Brown had just returned from a business trip in Mexico. The man said he wasn't sure if his boss had even spoken to anyone at the ranch.

"Mr. Brown will be in the Metroplex on Monday," Brown's assistant said in a nice and professional manner. "He has several meetings but I am sure he can meet with you, say about two o'clock."

Lowe's simple case of fraud was getting more confusing with each day that passed. He had no questions really about Brown being in Mexico when Double Ds Delight ate his last scoop of oats. He never figured he would have done the dirty deed himself anyway. He was finding it confusing that the man's assistant let on like the man didn't even know the horse was dead. It puzzled the officers for the remainder of the day.

Defoe had always told him to get away from a case for a while when it gets to the point where it is driving you crazy. Lowe was well past that point when he decided to take the ranger's advice.

It was Friday afternoon and he really couldn't do anything besides read the same reports until Monday. He already had the damn things memorized as it was. A weekend off seemed like the right thing to do. He thought Monday morning might give him a fresh set of eyes to view the case.

"Marcia it's me. David. I was wondering if you were serious about going riding. I was thinking about letting this case simmer for a few days," Lowe said when he called her.

"That's a good idea David. I was way serious about the riding. What about tomorrow?" she asked.

"It sounds good to me," he paused as an idea from his youth came to him.

"Marcia, when I was a kid, my granddaddy Albin used to take me out to the Grasslands to ride. I just now remembered it. "What do you say we pack us a lunch and take the horses? We can make a day out of it," Lowe suggested to her.

"And then Sunday we can go watch Kelly Sue show. We can make a whole weekend out of it," Selter said, enlarging the plans.

The day Lowe and Marcia Selter spent at the Grasslands was amazing. They spent the morning racing their ponies through an autumn meadow, stopping here and there to kiss. Young love was in bloom although the leaves on the Post Oak trees had begun to turn red and gold.

They ate lunch while talking and watching Meathead play by an old, cement water tank. The only thing wrong with the day was that it ended far too soon. A late afternoon shower chased the lovebirds away from the small piece of Texas paradise.

The next morning, the two got up at the crack of dawn and left for a small cutting horse event about two hours north of the state line. It was plain to see Kelly was happy to see them and prouder still to show off his pupil.

Kelly Sue was unlike any stereo, typically rich brat. She was respectful and considerate. Lowe couldn't help but think that maybe it was due to the influence of her horse trainer.

They all went out for lunch after the girl had shown her cutting horse. Kelly Sue and the Sheriff laughed while hearing Shawn tell stories of Lowe's younger days showing cutting horses.

"Do you miss it, David?" Selter asked.

"I did, just a little, before this old horse thief started telling those old stories," Lowe answered while laughing. "About half of them, I don't remember that way," he added.

Lowe and the Sheriff went home after the meal. They would have stayed longer but Kelly Sue had to catch a flight back to school later that evening.

All in all, it was the best weekend that Lowe could remember and not once did his case enter into the conversation. But like all good things, the weekend had to come to an end. Lowe and Meathead were back in their motel room by nine that evening.

Monday morning offered a renewed sense of resolve to the peace officer. The old ranger had been right about stepping away from the case. Lowe had a spring in his step as he prepared to meet the day

"Come on Meathead, time for your walk," Lowe told the pup.

He was busy trying to put the leash on the rambunctious, playful puppy when there came a knock at the door. Lowe's first thought was that it was Kelly. After all, the man had made a habit of showing up first thing in the morning. He expected the same line of questioning about the missing Garret Mise.

Lowe was surprised to find it was not Kelly on the other side of the door. A puzzled looked appeared on his face when he saw Dr. Jason Southerland was his visitor.

"What can I do for you this morning, Doctor," Lowe said pleasantly.

"I was wondering if any results came back yet on Double Ds Delight," the man asked.

Lowe could tell the man was on a fishing expedition. The question was why and who might have sent him? He didn't know what the Brown's vet was up to but he decided to play along.

"When was the last time you looked at the potency of the stud's semen," Lowe questioned.

"I don't know, maybe a year or two. I would have to check my records. Why?" Southerland answered.

"According to the autopsy, the horse was losing his potential as a viable breeding animal. I would think that if one had a stud with such value, his sperm count should be evaluated at the beginning of each breeding season. From what I know and read, it's standard procedure.

The man seemed to be stunned by Lowe's expertise. He assumed that Lowe couldn't cut it as a veterinarian and that was the reason he became a DPS officer.

"Normally you would be correct but Double D was sent to Kentucky the beginning of the breeding season. I knew they would run the sperm count test so I saw no need to run the same test twice," the vet replied, scrambling for an answer.

The vet then asked a question that made Lowe question Southerland's own veterinarian capabilities, asking why the test even mattered. Lowe was so taken aback that he almost asked the man to repeat the question, fearing he misunderstood Southerland.

"My God man, it offers motive," said a shocked Lowe. "You and I both know a stud that cannot cover a mare is nothing more than a pet. That is perfectly fine except for the fact that months before he goes completely sterile, he turns up not dead but killed. Now figure in a million-dollar-plus insurance policy and things get real suspicious." Lowe said, going line-by-line explaining why the reproductive test made a difference in his investigation.

"I see. If that is the case, what are you going to do next?" the Brown's veterinarian asked.

I have a meeting this afternoon in Dallas with Mr. Brown, if you must know," Lowe said, not meaning to be sharp with man but it was almost like Southerland was pumping him for information and he was tired of it.

"You're gonna meet Mr. Brown this afternoon; I thought he was out of the country," the veterinarian said, with his speech picking up pace.

"He's back and yes I am meeting with the man," Lowe repeated.

Lowe couldn't tell if the vet caught the hint he was becoming aggravated with all the questions or if he was just in a hurry to go after his last question. He told Lowe he had to go to see a colicking horse, but Lowe thought there might be more to it.

Lowe knew the question about "why the vet suddenly got in a hurry" would have to wait, along with all his other unanswered questions. They seemed to be piling up; more questions than answers.

Lowe had already arranged to drop Meathead off at Sheriff Selter's before going to his meeting with Brown. He should have been there a hour earlier and would have if not for Southerland's little visit.

"I was just about ready to send out a search party," Selter told him as he and his pup got out of the car.

"I am sorry, Marcia. Southerland showed with a truckload of questions. It was a strange way to start the day," Lowe explained

"That's about par, he's a strange man anyway," she let it be known.

"It was like he was looking for something," Lowe confided.

"Like what?" Selter asked.

"Who knows? Like you said, he's an odd duck," answered Lowe, agreeing with her earlier assessment.

The two talked for a while before Lowe left for his meeting with Mr. Brown. He thought about asking her to go with him but thought better of it since the interview was taking place in a gentlemen's club.

It wasn't that he thought she couldn't handle it; she was a professional. The question was if he could handle being in a strip club with his new girlfriend while trying to conduct an interview.

He thanked her for watching the pup while he was gone and promised to call her if anything came up.

"Now Meathead, you be good. Stay out of the flowerbeds and don't eat no saddles while I'm gone," Lowe said to the pup before he kissed the Sheriff goodbye.

The DPS officer was once again alone with his thoughts as he drove to his appointment. It had been one of the craziest months he could ever recall. Lowe had gone from being in Captain McDowell's doghouse to running his own investigation. It might have started out a run-of-the mill fraud case but it was turning into anything but run of the mill. His case had more twists and turns than a hip hop street dance.

He then thought of the beautiful Sheriff, Marcia Selter. It had been many years since he had anything like the feelings he was experiencing. He wondered if he had ever had such feelings. It seemed so right and they seemed so perfect together. Lowe wanted, more than anything else, for it to continue long after the case was in the books.

His mind wandered, right up to the time that he turned off the interstate. Lowe then had to turn his attention to finding the gentlemen's club for his meeting. Lowe just knew Lucius Defoe would have been laughing his ass off if he knew how quick his mind went from his new girlfriend to finding a strip club.

"All in the line of duty," he imagined the old ranger saying.

Lowe was on the road that the club was located on when two, then three, squad cars went speeding past him. "Damn, where's the fire?" he asked under his breath.

It didn't take but a few minutes for him to answer his own question. It wasn't just three squad cars. Like him, they were just late arrivals. Lowe had counted two DPS trooper units, two city units and one County Sheriff vehicle. They all had one thing in common: they were all in the club's parking lot where he was supposed to meet Brown.

The yellow crime tape was already up when Lowe got out of his car. Two city cops were posted to keep the on-looking crowd at bay. One told him to get back before he had the chance to flash his badge.

"Sorry, Officer Lowe," the man apologized.

"That's alright son, you were doing you job. What do we have, Officer Powers," Lowe asked, reading the man's nameplate.

"A hit and run, sir," the policeman answered.

"Some guy got jealous of his old lady and ran down one of the patrons?" Lowe asked, taking a guess.

"No sir, it was the owner," the officer reported.

"I'll be a son-of-.... Where is the lead officer," Lowe asked bluntly.

"Over there by the victim. His name is Lieutenant Dickerson," the man said pointing in the direction where group of men stood.

"Who is Dickerson?" Lowe asked approaching the group of four officers.

"That would be me. And you are?" the Lieutenant wanted to know.

"Officer David Lowe of the DPS. Is that John Brown," Lowe asked looking down at the covered body.

"Yep, the King of Silicon. Did you know the man?" asked the Lieutenant, answering Lowe's question then asking one of his own.

"Nope, but I had an appointment with him concerning a case I am working," he told the Lieutenant.

"You think it might be related?" was the man's next question.

"I don't have a clue. Why don't you fill me in Lieutenant and maybe I can answer that for you," Lowe offered.

The Lieutenant began to tell Lowe what was known. He told Lowe that Brown had gone to his car to retrieve some papers. A late-model pickup truck was lying in wait and ran the man over. It was all the Lieutenant knew at the time.

"Did anyone get a description of the pickup?" Lowe asked

"Hey Danny, bring Officer Lowe that description of the truck," Lieutenant Dickerson ordered.

Lowe couldn't believe his eyes, but there it was, right down to the Arkansas plates.

"I was just fixing to put a APB out on it," the Lieutenant told Lowe.

"Don't bother, I put one out on the same truck two weeks ago," Lowe informed the man.

"So it is related to your case. I'll tell you what Lowe, if you state boys want it, I have no problem kicking it up to you," the Lieutenant said.

"I can't make that decision Lieutenant, it's above my pay grade. Let me call my Captain and see what he thinks," Lowe replied.

He stepped away from the noise and confusion to put in the call to headquarters.

"Captain our case just went from fraud to murder," Lowe told McDowell who was listening on the other end of the line.

What do you mean, did you find the Mise kid's body?" the Captain asked, remembering the conversation they had before.

"Nope, somebody ran Brown down before I had a chance to interview the man. Sir here's the kicker:

the vehicle in question matches Mise's truck perfectly. The locals want to know if we want the case," he informed McDowell.

"Damn Lowe, what did we step into? Tell them city boys we'll take it from here," the Captain ordered.

"Captain how long are we gonna have it? I'll bet a week's pay the G-men are already on their way up here," Lowe predicted.

"You let me worry about the Feds. You just work the case and try to get out of there before they show up," came another order.

"That ought be easy enough, the locals have most of the leg work already done. I'll just collect their notes. I do want to question Brown's personal assistant. I think I can do that before the suits show," Lowe advised the Captain.

"Quit yapping on the phone son and get it done," came the Captain's final order.

Lowe went back to where he had left the Lieutenant. He wanted to convey his Captain's feelings on jurisdiction and ask the whereabouts of Brown's assistant.

"His personal assistant? You must be talking about Mr. Miles," the Lieutenant said looking at his notes.

"I guess; I don't think I ever caught his name," Lowe explained.

"It says right here: Gary Miles. I remember now, he's the one that seems the most shook up. I suppose he is in the office. We haven't released anyone yet, so that would be my guess," said the Lieutenant.

"If you don't mind gathering all your people's notes while I go talk with Miles, I would be grateful," Lowe said politely.

"I don't mind at all, if it means you all are doing the paperwork on this one," the man joked.

"Everybody knows how much we love paperwork," Lowe joked right back before going to find Mr. Miles.

It wasn't hard to see the Lieutenant had been right about the man's emotional state. Lowe found the man pacing the floor in Brown's office. He could tell by the reddening of Miles's eyes he had been crying.

"Mr. Miles, I am officer Lowe. I spoke to you on Friday," he reminded the man.

"Officer Lowe it's all my fault, I should have gone to the car for Mr. Brown," the man repeated two or three times.

"I don't think so Mr. Miles; I don't think that would have made a difference at all. This was planned and if you would have gone to the car, more than likely the killer would have waited until Mr. Brown exited the club," Lowe reasoned, trying to calm the man down.

Miles repeated his assertion again. Lowe, in desperation, finally went to the bar and asked for a stiff drink for the troubled man. He then returned to the office and asked the man to have a seat.

"Here Mr. Miles, have a drink to settle you. Then perhaps I can ask you a few questions," Lowe instructed the man.

Lowe looked for a chair for himself as he waited for the drink to have its desired effect. He thought if he sat in Brown's chair it would just upset Miles even more.

Lowe found a chair by the door with a silver-belly cowboy hat hanging on the back of it. He respectfully picked the hat up from its resting place. Lowe could tell it belonged to the late John Brown. It didn't take a lot of deduction skills to reach his conclusion. The inside of the hat read, "Custom made for John Brown, by JW Brooks."

"Damn, they do make a nice hat," Lowe said to himself.

"Did you tell Mr. Brown the reason why I wanted to talk to him?' Lowe asked after the man had finished his drink.

"I did, he was just as surprised as I was. He was looking forward to getting the details from you Officer Lowe," the man answered.

"Do you know if he called the ranch to inquire about the horse's death?" was Lowe's next question.

"I don't think so. Like I said, he wanted to talk with you first," Miles repeated.

"That is very strange, I would have thought his lawyer, Mr. Thigpen, would have called him when I questioned Mrs. Brown," Lowe said out loud.

"Thigpin, who is Thigpin?" Miles asked. "Mr. Brown's attorney is Monty Mitchell out of Houston. I have never heard of the other guy."

The man's answer blew Lowe's mind. He never figured on the Browns having two different lawyers. He knew the best assumption was the Browns were having marriage problems. He also knew the spouse of the victim was always on top of the suspect list. However, he couldn't figure out how Garret Mise figured into the equation. Now his murder case was just as confusing as the fraud case had been.

After asking the usual questions, Lowe asked Brown's personal assistant for the phone number of the attorney in Houston. They were questions like, "Has anyone had been making any threats" or "Was Brown having any financial problems?" They were questions anyone who watched an hour of television would know to ask.

"I want to thank you Mr. Miles for being so helpful in this time of need. Let me see if I can't give you a ride back to your hotel room. If I have anymore questions, can I reach you at the number I reached you on Friday?" Lowe asked before walking the man out to his car.

"Yes sir, I'll be back in the office tomorrow making the arrangements for Mr. Brown," Miles told Lowe.

Lowe was busy telling Lieutenant Dickerson what the man had said when another officer interrupted the conversation.

"Lieutenant, they found the truck that run over our victim over in Fort Worth. They say it was abandoned near the Stock Yards off of Exchange Avenue," the officer said to the Lieutenant.

"Don't tell me, tell officer Lowe. It's his baby now," Dickerson pointed out.

"Did you ask them not to tow it off until I get there?" Lowe asked the officer who had reported the news.

"It's been a pleasure, Lieutenant Dickerson," Lowe said before turning to head for his car.

Lowe had been right about the FBI. He spied agents Swink and Diggs through his rearview mirror before driving away.

"Have fun, boys," he said, where only he could hear.

Lowe made good use of his time while he made the one-hour drive across the Metroplex. First he called the office of the Fort Worth DPS and asked if they had a crime technician who could meet him at the scene of the abandoned pickup. After securing their help, he called Sheriff Selter.

"Hey Marcia, it's me. I am gonna be hung up here until who knows when. John Brown just got himself killed. I was hoping I could get you to make the next-of-kin notification. I don't know what time I'm gonna make it back. Besides, I don't think Mrs. Brown cares too much for me," he said to the Sheriff.

"I don't know why, as good-looking and charming as you are," Selter said with a playful sound in her voice.

"Do you want me to go by and tell Shawn?' she asked with a more serious tone.

"No, he is at a sale. I'll go by there when I get back and tell him," was Lowe's answer.

They talked until the batteries in his cellphone finally gave out. He told her about the hit and run and that Mise's truck was used in the commission of the crime. It threw her off as much as it did him when he first found out.

She told him not to worry about Meathead. He could pick the pup up the next morning if he wanted to. Lowe thanked her and then the cellphone went dead. He was just about to tell her how much he missed her but never got the chance.

Lowe relieved the Fort Worth police officer who had been guarding the abandoned truck. Ten minutes later, the crime tech from the DPS office showed up. Together he and Lowe went through the vehicle with a fine-tooth comb.

However, all of their attention to detail yielded very little in the way of evidence. It was what they didn't find that was eye popping. They found one set of prints on everything: the cassettes, radio and dash. Lowe figured they belonged to the missing Mise. What they didn't find were any prints on the steering wheel or door handle. Lowe could tell they had been wiped clean.

The sun had long since disappeared into the west when he finally made it back to Whitesboro. Lowe's first thought was to keep driving until he was in Gainesville, back at his motel. The day had been so long, he had almost forgotten how it had started.

Lowe did not give into his need for rest. Instead he stayed the course. He wanted to break the news about Brown to Shawn Kelly himself. He knew Kelly had been at a horse sale in Oklahoma City. The chances were he too was just getting home.

He was right because the lights were still on in the house when he drove up. Kelly was a creature of habit. If not for the sale, he would have been in bed hours earlier. Lowe knew this when he knocked at the door.

"Come on in, David. I was just making me a drink; you want one?" Kelly asked after inviting his friend in.

"Hell yes! Whatever you're making, make mine twice as strong," Lowe told the man.

"I guess it's been that kind of day old buddy?" Kelly questioned.

"You don't know the half of it," Lowe replied.

Lowe thought it might be best to hold off on the bad news until they had the first drink. He didn't know whose best interests it would serve but it was the strategy he followed.

"Shawn I have some good news, bad news and worse news. How would you like it?" Lowe asked after their first drink.

"Straight up, just like our whiskey," the horse trainer answered.

"The good news is, we found Garret Mise's pickup. The bad news is, John Brown was run over today and killed. And the worse new is, it was Mise's truck that ran over Brown," Lowe said laying his cards on the table.

"I don't believe it; the boy is no killer," said an enraged Kelly rising from his chair. "He just doesn't have it in him."

"Calm down Shawn; damn it. I didn't say Mise murdered Brown. I said his truck ran the man down. You remember what the old fart used to always say, 'There's many a slip between a cup and a lip.'

"If it is any help, I'm not so sure Mise did it either. The alternative; however, is just as grim. You wanted it straight, so here's the way I see it: if Mise didn't kill Brown, the chances are real good that the boy is dead himself. For all I know, he's at the bottom of Lake Ray Hubbard," said Lowe, voicing his thoughts to the man for the first time.

Kelly sank back down in his chair. The room fell silent as the horse trainer processed what he had just been told.

"If you don't think Garret did it, then who? Who killed Garret and to what end?" questioned Kelly after a measure of time had passed.

"Hell Shawn, if I new that, I wouldn't be over here wanting another drink more than I wanted Marcia's sweet touch. Every time I think I have a grip on this freaking case, it gets away from me.

You could fill a textbook with all the theories I've had shot out from under me," Lowe confessed to the man.

"Is it true what you said about wanting another drink?" Kelly asked, rising from his chair once more.

"You're damn right and make it just like the last one," came Lowe's request.

Lowe only thought he wanted another drink. What he was really craving was sleep. Kelly knew that was the case when he returned and found his friend sound asleep in the chair. Kelly threw a blanket over Lowe and turned out the light.

CHAPTER 8

OFF TO SEE THE RANGER

After the death of John Brown, Lowe spent the morning trying to get a crick out of his neck. It was the price he had to pay for falling asleep in a chair at Kelly's house. The crick was the first thing he noticed, the second was the time.

Half of the morning was wasted by the time he got Meathead rounded up and he had driven back to the motel for a shower. It was the first time Lowe could remember wishing Kelly had woke him up earlier.

He could only guess his oldest friend thought he could use the rest. Kelly might have been right about the rest but still the biggest part of the morning was lost to him.

Lowe was cleaning out his shirt pockets when he found the number to Brown's attorney in Houston. It seemed like a good place to start his work for the day on the case. With his phone in hand, he put in a call to Monty Mitchell, the lawyer for the deceased.

Earlier that morning Mitchell had been notified by Brown's assistant of his client's sudden death.

"Mr. Mitchell I don't want to take up a lot of your time but I do have a few questions for you," Lowe told the lawyer after introducing himself.

"I'll do my best to answer them, but please understand that legally I am limited on what I can tell you. John Brown might be dead but he is still due the confidentiality the law allows," Mitchell said.

Lowe began by asking about Brown's business dealings. He knew most of the questions wouldn't be answered but he still had to ask. He found out very little information with that line of questioning, so he moved on to the personal questions.

Mitchell did confirm that there was a prenuptial agreement signed by Mrs. Brown and then he briefly outlined the contents. The agreement said: "In the event of a divorce, Mrs. Brown would only receive a quarter-of-a-million-dollar payout."

"What about in the case of death?" Lowe asked.

"Then fifty percent of Brown's wealth would revert to Mrs. Brown. The rest would be placed in trust for the daughter," the lawyer replied.

"I know you can't tell me the overall value of the estate, but could you ballpark it for me?" Lowe asked.

"Not having the numbers in front of me, I would guess between twenty-five and thirty million," came the man's estimate.

"Just between you and me Mr. Mitchell, that's a whole lot of motive," Lowe expressed.

"Since I only represent the estate, not Mrs. Brown, I tend to agree," Mitchell confided. "This will take sometime going through probate. I would appreciate being kept in the loop if you find evidence of foul play," the lawyer added.

Lowe told Mitchell it would be up to his Captain but he would do his best. He went on to ask a few follow-up questions before bringing the conversation to an end.

His next phone call was to Sheriff Selter. He hadn't been able to talk to her that morning because he had overslept. She had already gone into the office when he had picked up his pup.

His reasons for calling her were many, both professional and personal. He wanted to thank her once again for watching Meathead the day before and tell her he was thinking of her. He could only guess she already knew the second part as well as he did.

"The man who thinks he knows a woman's mind, is a fool," he remembered reading somewhere.

He remembered the quote, not because he had any questions about Selter's thoughts or feelings. He thought of it because of JJ Brown. Selter had made the death notification the night before. Lowe wondered what her thoughts were on the way the woman reacted to the news.

A man may not know a woman's mind but perhaps another woman would. It seemed to be a logical, as well as a professional, path to pursue.

"A good morning to you, Officer Lowe," came Selter's normally sweet voice over the phone.

"It's morning, but not by much. I am sorry I missed you this morning; I kinda over slept," Lowe explained.

"Yes I know. Shawn called me earlier. He said you were dead tired last night and he didn't have the heart to wake you up this morning," she recounted.

"Anyway, I picked up Meathead and once again I wanted to think you for keeping a eye on him for me," he told her.

"It seemed like the least I could do after pawning him off on you," she said with a laugh.

"Yes you did, but look at all the benefits the little mutt came with. In saying that, I wanted to tell you that I missed seeing you last night. I know Sunday was only a few days ago but it seems like it's been a month," he said, speaking from his heart.

"Well handsome, if you come by tonight, I'll make it up to you," she offered.

"You can count me in. But that's if no one gets killed today. That brings me to my next question," said Lowe. "It seems like Mrs. Brown could have had fifteen million reasons for wanting Mr. Brown dead. I was wondering how she reacted when you gave her the bad news?" he wanted to know.

She thought for a moment before answering his question. "She seemed genuinely shocked but her grief seemed a bit over the top and forced. You know as well as I do, impressions one might have on another's grief are iffy at best," she said to him.

"I know, but sometimes impressions are all you got. I trust yours and feel it's worth looking into," Lowe explained.

"Didn't you tell me the witness said it was a man driving?" she asked.

"Yes, but it wouldn't be the first time someone farmed out a murder. Lord knows she can afford it.

"I think we need to get a look at her credit card, bank and phone records. I'll give Captain McDowell a call and see if he can't get us a warrant for them. Maybe the 'who done it' is in there," Lowe suggested.

"It's a starting point," she added.

"A starting point! After a month we have a starting point," he mused.

"Tell me what he says over dinner tonight," she said in a voice that was inviting.

Lowe was just about to call Captain McDowell when his phone rang. It was Defoe on the other end. He had nearly forgotten the request he had made of his friend after everything that had taken place in the past twenty-four hours.

"Hey boy, how's it hanging?" came the ranger's greeting.

"I'm up to my ass in alligators, Lucius," Lowe replied.

"I've been there. Why don't you jump ship and come down to the ranch tomorrow, I've got a man with some eye-opening information for you," the old ranger told him.

"I would loved to Lucius but I am gonna have to call the Captain first. Our principle reason for wanting to look behind the curtain of the FBI was turned into road-kill yesterday. I've got to see if the Captain still has the hankering to find out what they won't tell us," Lowe told Defoe.

"Well son, if you see how it all started, you might be able to see where it's headed," Defoe explained.

"I can't say you don't have a point. I'll convey it to the big man. I was just fixing to call McDowell anyway. Stay close to the phone. I'll let you know what he says," Lowe requested.

"10-4 on that, I'm knee deep in paper work and I ain't going anywhere for a while," the ranger answered with a laugh.

Lowe called headquarters the minute he got off the phone with Defoe. He started by telling McDowell his latest theory of the case. He then requested the warrant for Mrs. Brown's financials and phone records. The Captain agreed it was worth the warrant and said he would get it to him.

"Captain, I just got off the phone with Lucius. He wants me to come down there and meet with a man about the reason we can't get the Feds to cooperate. I told him I'd have to check with you and see if it's something you want me to pursue now that Brown's dead. Lucius said it might offer us some context," Lowe reported.

"Defoe might have something there and I still want to find out what the FBI is hiding. It's gonna take a day or two to get the warrant and then get the computer tech to gather the records," said McDowell.

"You go on down there and see what Defoe's man has to say. I'll have all the records sent to your motel room when we get them," McDowell ordered.

Once again his case was going to take him miles away from the beautiful Marcia Selter. But that was before he had an idea.

He called the ranger back and told him McDowell had given him the thumbs up on the trip. He then asked Defoe if he minded if he brought someone with him. He told the ranger it was someone he was working the case with; he left out the rest.

Lowe called the Sheriff after getting the okay from Defoe.

"Don't tell me you're calling to cancel dinner?" she asked in a disappointed tone.

"No, not for all the money in the world. I was calling to see if you could get away for a few days. My friend, the ranger I was telling you about, has a guy who would like to talk to us about the case tomorrow. I was thinking two heads were better than one," he explained to her.

"Is that the only reason you want me to go?" Selter asked.

"What do you think?" he countered with a tinge of mischief in his voice.

"I guess I could get Gracy to tend my critters. Yes David, I think I would like to go," was her answer.

The two set off early the next morning for South Texas. They had made an agreement the night before that they would talk about anything but the case on the way to Defoe's.

The case was the reason why they were going; naturally they would discuss it while there. And they would more than likely talk about it on the way home. The six-hour drive to Defoe's ranch was theirs and that was the agreement.

The first hour he spent telling her about the old ranger and how from the shadows, he had watched Lowe grow to be a man.

"I loved my grandfather, don't get me wrong. The man just had funny ways. I guess we all do. He hated anything to do with the DPS after my parents were killed and that included Lucius," Lowe said, describing his grandfather's fight with the department.

"It was his way of dealing with the loss," Selter offered.

Lowe went on to tell her about the one case that he and Defoe had worked together. He couldn't tell her everything because some details he would have to take to the grave. It was legal; just not in that century.

"Lucius is old school but a person could learn a lot from the old ways," he declared.

The way Lowe talked about the old ranger made it easy for her to figure out. Defoe was the father figure he never had and Lowe idolized the man. She was sure she knew Defoe by the time the topic changed.

Selter took the lead in the conversation for a while. She told him about Midnight, her first pony. Her daddy had traded a plow mule for the little horse.

"He always said it was the best trade he ever made because of the smile I had on my face the first time I saw Midnight." By the way she spoke of her father and the pony, he could tell it was a special time in her life.

"I remember my first pony, a mean little cuss, but I loved him," Lowe shared. "I used to pretend I was Matt Dillon riding in to save Dodge City. I was doing just that when Lucius and Ranger Jackson came to tell us how my folks were killed. My Lord, I haven't thought of that in years."

It was late afternoon when they arrived at the gate of the Cinco Peso Ranch. Lowe told Selter that the first Texas Ranger badges were made from the silver cinco peso. Defoe had named his ranch to honor the heritage of the oldest law enforcement agency in America.

They drove up the dirt road that cut through the pasture and led to the ranger's house. The first humans they saw were an old black man and a much younger white man sitting on the veranda.

"Ranger Defoe is a lot younger than I thought he would be," Selter committed.

Lowe laughed, "That's Kolt Kersh, he's the local Sheriff, from a county over. The other man is Pop Johnson. He kinda runs the place. Come on, I'll introduce you," he said while getting out of the car.

"It's about time you showed up David; we was running out of lies to tell each other," Kersh said as both men stood up.

"Hell I took a wrong turn at the third cow patty," Lowe joked. "Boys I would like to introduce you to Sheriff Marcia Selter from Whitesboro," he continued after his try at some South Texas humor.

Both men removed their cowboy hats and held out their hands, as was the custom.

"My, my, we's gots the prettiest Sheriff in Texas at ours little ranch," the old black man marveled.

"It looks like we have Texas's tallest Sheriff too," Selter said while looking up at the six-foot-six Kersh.

"Where's that old, sorry excuse of a ranger?" Lowe asked referring to Defoe.

"Old Jefferson, he done got himself a runny nose. The Captain, he'd be out at the barn trying to gives that mangy, old buffalo a shot," Pop answered.

"You mean you two ain't lending a hand?" Lowe wondered.

"The last time I's try to help with the Captain's two-thousand-pound pet, I's stove up for a week," Pop pointed out.

"What about you, Kolt?" Lowe asked the other man.

"Hell David, someone has got to be able to dial 9-1-1," the man said with a laugh. "No seriously, I offered but you know how pigheaded Lucius is when it comes to Jefferson," Kersh stated.

"Well, I think I'll walk back there and see if we need to dig a grave or not. Marcia, do you want to come," Lowe invited.

"You two just fire your weapons three times in the air if you run into trouble. Me and Pop, we'll come a running," Kersh laughed as Lowe and Selter headed for the barn.

"I didn't know Defoe held the rank of Captain in the rangers," Selter said on the way.

"I don't think you could give Lucius the rank of Captain. Pop calls any white man with a badge Captain. I reckon it was all the years he spent on the prison farm. Defoe and Jackson talked the Governor into pardoning the old man after he'd been there twenty years too long. Pop has been with Lucius ever since," Lowe explained.

"An ex-convict and a stray buffalo. Defoe must have a kind heart," she stated seeing the real beauty of the ranger.

"That's Lucius, he never saw a stray he didn't bring home. Somewhere around here, there's a pack of dogs he's collected over the years. I imagine they're either with him or down at the tank," Lowe told her.

They found the ranger and his American bison in one of the holding pens. Defoe was a sight with his denim shirt ripped and covered in Buffalo mucus; all the by-products of his misadventure.

"You knew I was coming; why didn't you wait?" Lowe said scolding the old ranger. "Despite what they say, I am a pretty fair vet."

I know, but Jefferson is a little particular," the ranger spoke with his back toward them.

"Hell he can't be that particular, he's here ain't he? And where's that pack of dogs of yours?" Lowe asked. "I figured they would have been making this fiasco a bit more interesting."

"They would have to, but I penned them up. Son, I am just a little smarter than I look," Defoe came back.

"Come here you old coot, I've got someone here I want you to meet," Lowe yelled to the man with his back turned.

"Hold your horses, I just about got this whipped," Defoe yelled back.

Defoe hadn't turned to face them up until that point. He had no inclination who Lowe had brought with him. The ranger figured Lowe was bringing one of his fellow officers. He indicated it was someone he was working the case with.

The old ranger's eye widened when he saw the beautiful Sheriff Selter at Lowe's side.

"Pardon me ma'am; I didn't realize young David was bringing someone as lovely as you," Defoe said removing his hat.

"Lucius, I would like you to meet Sheriff Marcia Selter; we are working the case together," said Lowe, making the introductions.

"Ranger Defoe, I feel like I already know you. David speaks of you often," she said with a smile.

"Well, Sheriff, that could be a good thing or a bad thing. It all depends on what set of lies he has told you," joked the ranger as he opened the gate for the buffalo.

It was like a huge mass of hide and hair was being launched from a cannon, the way Jefferson shot through the gap between the posts.

"I won't see him for a month, ungrateful cuss," Defoe hollered at the backside of the bison.

"Some things never change around here, Lucius," Lowe committed

"And some things do," Defoe said while washing up in the barn out of Selter's hearing range.

"She's a hell of a cop, Lucius," Lowe bragged.

"And a damn good-looking cop, to boot," the ranger added.

"You noticed that." Lowe laughed.

"Damn son, I am one of Texas's finest," Defoe fired back.

"You want me to turn these dogs loose?" Lowe offered.

" No, I'll get Pop to do it. I don't want to overwhelm her with my canine welcome wagon.

We best get back outside; we can't leave her standing in the sun," Defoe told his young friend.

The two men walked out of the barn to find her petting one of the ranger's mounts. The two men marveled at the way she had with the three-year-old.

"She'll work," was about all Defoe could say.

Lucius Defoe had spent nearly a quarter century as a Texas Ranger and not a lot got past him. He could tell from the first few minutes around his guest, there was something else there besides the case. It was the way Lowe looked at her; the way she followed his gaze. It didn't take much of a detective to know the two were in love. He just wondered if they knew it yet.

It wasn't long before everyone was back on the veranda. It turned out that Kursh had volunteered to help Pop with the cooking. Lowe always looked forward to seeing the South Texas Sheriff.

"I don't know about anyone else but I could use a beer. Kolt, why don't you get us a round out of the ice box," Defoe suggested.

"I hate to say it Lucius, but you could also use a shower," Kersh pointed out.

"Amen to that Captain. You's a lot better downs wind," Pop said putting in his two cents.

"Let me get a brew poured down my throat and I'll do just that. Pop when you go out to feed, would you turn the dogs loose?" the ranger asked of the man.

"I'll get to it, Captain," Pop replied, leaving his seat on the veranda.

"Lucius, you said you had a man who wanted to meet with us concerning our case?" Lowe inquired while Kursh was retrieving the beer from inside.

"I did, Danny Head, a former field supervisor for the FBI in El Paso," the ranger told him.

Lowe couldn't help but start laughing.

"What's so funny, boy?" Defoe wanted to know.

"I just acquired a pup named Meathead, I just thought they might be related," Lowe said still laughing.

"I am glad you got that out of your system before the man showed up and got offended," the ranger said trying not to break into laughter himself.

"Well Lucius, where is Mr. Head?" Lowe asked trying not to laugh.

"I sent Trooper Johnson to San Antonio to pick him up at the airport. They ought to be here in an hour or so. You remember Alvin, don't you," Defoe asked referring to Trooper Johnson.

"Yes sir, one of the finest DPS officers the state of Texas ever put on the road," Lowe complimented.

"I'll drink to that," Kursh said as he passed out the beer.

"Listen to this Kolt. David finally got himself a dog. A dog named Meathead, must be a hell of a junkyard dog with a handle like that," Defoe stated.

"He's just a pup, but he's got all the makings," Lowe reported.

"I'm sorry Sheriff, would you just listen to us go on; just like a pen of old roosters. It ain't often we get a lady out here. There's a restroom inside if you need to freshen up," Defoe told his guest.

"Lucius, I told you, you're the one who needs to freshen up," Kursh said repeating his earlier statement.

"Alright, alright, I'm going," the old ranger said, giving into the request of the mob.

Texas Ranger Lucius Defoe was everything Selter thought he would be and more. He looked liked he had just walked out of central casting and able to play the good guy in any old black-and-white movie. It seemed to her if James A. Michener was looking for a character to write about, Defoe would be his man.

"Is he always so, you know, Western?" she asked the two men still remaining on the veranda.

"Pretty much, but don't let that old ranger fool you. When it comes to the law, he's second to none," Lowe advised her.

"I second that," Kursh said holding out his bottle to toast the ranger.

Forty-five minutes later, a cleaner and a much-better smelling Defoe was back outside with his guest. Kursh had gone around back to help Pop with building a fire for their meal. A cloud of dust appeared coming toward the house.

"That would be Alvin," Defoe said rising from his chair.

Lowe and Defoe walked out to meet the black-and-white, state-issued unit.

Trooper Johnson parked next to Lowe's vehicle in the driveway. Defoe's driveway was beginning to look like a car lot or a cop convention. Kursh was quick to point that out when he came around the house.

A man, who looked to be the same age as Defoe, got out on the passenger's side. It wasn't hard to see the man had once been a Fed. He still looked the part, from his cheap blue suit to his wingtip shoes.

"How are you doing Danny? I hope you had a nice flight," Defoe said while greeting the man.

"I almost forgot how desolate this part of the world is," Head committed after taking in the emptiness of that part of Texas.

"Awe Danny, not everyone can retire to the 'plushness' of New England. Come on up to the house and I'll get you a cold one so you can wash some of that Texas dust out of your throat.

You two boys get the man's gear," Defoe instructed Lowe and Johnson.

"I see you're still doing Defoe's leg work, Alvin," Lowe said in a playful tone.

"That's me, Tonto, to the Lone Derange Ranger," the man joked right back.

"I heard that," Defoe yelled from the veranda.

All the gear that the former Fed had with him was a battered, old briefcase. Evidently Head didn't plan to stay long. Lowe could deduct from his attitude he'd be on the next flight out.

"My God Lucius, what in the hell happened to bring all you law-enforcement people together,"

Head asked after being introduced to officer Lowe. Two Texas Sheriffs and then there was Defoe and Alvin.

"David and Sheriff Selter are the two who need to talk to you. The rest of us are just bystanders fixing to eat us a steak," Defoe explained.

"Let's get to it, as you are fond of saying in Texas," the man said opening his briefcase, taking out an old file.

"What's this?" Lowe asked after being handed the folder.

"It's everything you need to know about the life and times of Johnny O'Neal," Head told him.

Lowe first thought he misunderstood the man who spoke with a heavy Boston ascent. He then became confused when he read the name on the outside of the file. He even briefly wondered if he and the Sheriff had driven all that way for nothing.

"I think there has been some mistake. I inquired about a fellow named John Brown. I have never heard of Johnny O'Neal," Lowe said, first looking at Head and then Defoe.

"Nope, there's no mistake. You see in the 80s, Johnny O'Neal was a Lieutenant in the Irish mob. They said he was a whiz when it came to numbers. The bosses had turned all the accounting over to O'Neal. It made sense to keep it inhouse.

"In '85, he got pinched by the agency and was looking at some serious time. All his loyalties kind of went out the window and he cut a deal. O'Neal wasn't your normal run-of-the-mill hood; this cat was slick.

"He told the agency he had all the goods on the mob and if they were willing to play ball, he would tell them where all the bodies were buried. The higher ups jumped at the chance and made the deal with the devil.

"The deal he struck was a stroke of genius, if nothing else. O'Neal wanted a new identity for him and his wife, as well as a new location. In exchange, he would give the Justice Department a few names a year and testify against those people. He always had a hold card by not giving it all up at once," Head recounted.

"In other words, he had the government by the short hairs," Defoe interjected.

"Let me get this right, O'Neal and Brown are one in the same," Lowe reasoned out loud.

"Yes, but that's only half the story," continued Head. "O'Neal being the bookkeeper for the mob, left with a boat load of their money. Some estimates say he left with over two-million dollars.

"He laid low for awhile, then he set out building his own organization. The first move he made was to go into business with your old buddy Sanchez, Lucius. You see all the money they made trafficking drugs, they laundered through the strip joints," the former FBI agent continued by starting to unravel Brown's secret life.

"What about the apparent suicide of Jane Brown," Sheriff Selter wanted to know.

"From what I've been able to gather, everyone knew that Brown killed her in a fit of rage," said Head. "It was the first dilemma the agency faced with their informer. They could have arrested and charged Brown, but that meant the cases concerning the Irish mob would slide, so they covered it up and looked the other way - just the first of many black eyes the FBI would receive in the venture," the man said as he shook his head in disappointment.

"It's kinda like that old story: a man was walking above the timberline when he found a snake half froze. He picks up the creature and carries him down to his cabin. The man thaws out the snake by the warm fire and nurses him back to health. He then picks up the snake and gets bit. The man asks the creature why he had bit him after all he had done for him. You knew I was a snake when you picked me up, the snake replied," Defoe related, summing up what the retired agent was feeling.

"Can you tell me anything about the wiretap; why the Feds won't let us listen to it?" Lowe asked Head.

"Brown began to run out of names after a decade or so," began Head. "By then, it was plain to see he had created in Texas what he had been so instrumental in destroying on the East Coast. His drug ring had grown into a multi-million-dollar operation. The agency couldn't look the other way any longer.

"Brown was slippery though; it was going to be hard to find something that would stick. Brown and

Sanchez briefly had a third partner they cut out of the operation when they didn't need him anymore. No one even knew the third party existed until he anonymously contacted the agency. He was pissed that he was cut out and wanted some payback.

"The FBI were in secret negations with the man when the voice appeared on the wiretap. Some thought the voice belonged to the same man. They couldn't investigate it themselves without tipping their hand so they did the next best thing: they enlisted you guys to ferret out the information. The last thing they wanted was another situation like they had created with Brown.

"That's about it but I don't know what difference it makes. I heard before I left that Brown had been killed," Head noted.

"Well, it might make the Captain feel better knowing what the Feds were trying to hide. We still have a murder case to solve, no matter how dirty Brown was," Lowe stated

"You don't think the mob and his crooked deals caught up with him?" Defoe asked.

"I don't see it. It doesn't explain the fraud case I was working, or the Mise kid's truck being used in the homicide, not unless the mob started hiring eighteen-year-old ridge runners as hit men. Whoever laid Double Ds Delight low, more than likely did the same to John Brown," Lowe concluded.

As everyone began to go inside for supper, Lowe thanked Head for coming all that way to read him into the case. They all would return to the veranda hours later for a nightcap before officer Johnson took Head to his motel in town.

"The older you get, the longer the days become. I'm just about to end this one," Defoe said before turning in.

Lowe found the old ranger in the kitchen making coffee early the next morning.

"Where's the Sheriff?" Defoe wanted to know after asking the younger man how he had slept.

"She's in the shower," Lowe answered.

"She seems like a keeper boy; don't let her get away," Defoe said while pouring Lowe a cup of 'joe.'

"Why Lucius, I don't have any idea what you are talking about," he half-heartedly resisted.

"Bullshit, I am old but not blind. Don't do what I did and let this job consume you. I know our work is important but for Heaven's sake have a life. Have some kids and leave something behind besides a pile of paper work," said the ranger offering the younger man his advice, advice that rang for hours in Lowe's ears.

It was the old ranger's words that kept the ride on the way back to North Texas almost silent. The Sheriff thought that might be the case that was keeping her lover quiet.

"What are you thinking?" she probed an hour and a half away from home.

"Marcia do you mind if we make a little detour? There is something I'd like to show you." he said thoughtfully.

"No, what is it?" she asked.

"Just something up here a piece," Lowe said with a smile.

A few minutes later, he turned down a farm-to-market Road. Lowe brought the car to a stop at a gate about five miles down the road.

"I hope Massey ain't took to locking this gate," he said as he got out of the car to open it.

He found the gate wasn't locked so he opened it and drove through. Down the old dirt trail they went, through a cow pasture and then up a steep grade. On top of the hill, he stopped and got out. Sheriff Selter followed his lead not knowing what to expect.

"The people around these parts call this Hog Mountain. My granddaddy Albin used to bring me up here when I was a kid. Over there used to be an old domino shake. He and his friends would gather up here about twice a week and play moon and forty-two.

"This was our special place. He always told me, anything worth saying, could be said up here," Lowe explained before taking her hand.

"Marcia, the last month with you has been special, kinda like this place. I don't want it to end when the case does. I don't want it to end because I have fallen head over heals in love with you," said Lowe baring his soul.

It was at that point she knew why he had been so quiet that day. She already knew without a doubt that she loved him. She knew it after the first time they had met over lunch in Denton.

"I love you too," she said as she fell into his arms. "What took you so long and why now?" she asked after a long, wet kiss.

"You might say I got a little nudge by a much better detective then me," he said with a laugh before kissing her again.

CHAPTER 9

SHAKESPEARIAN NIGHTMARE

Lowe awoke for the first time in Selter's bed. It was the morning after he revealed his true feelings. He finally grasped the meaning of the old saying, "It's the first day of the rest of your life," the moment he opened his eyes.

He rolled over to find she was missing from her side of the bed. In the distance, he could hear the shower running. It dawned on him the world was moving along. She had her job and he had a case to solve. It didn't matter how much he wanted to stay in bed. He knew he couldn't. The job wouldn't allow it, and at that moment, Meathead wouldn't either. The pup kept barking at him from the floor in the room.

"Alright, alright I get the message. You want to go out side don't you?" Lowe said to the pup.

Selter was already cooking breakfast when Lowe returned from walking the pup.

"Morning Glory," she said as she fried up the bacon.

"And she cooks too. Meathead, I think we might have found the perfect woman," he said, laughing before kissing her.

"Do you have a busy day planned?" she asked.

"Unfortunately, I do. I called the Captain while Meathead did his business. He told me he sent up the financials covered in our warrant. They ought to be waiting in my motel room," he informed her.

"That sounds like a lot of fun," She said not really meaning it.

"You want to help?" he asked, already knowing the answer.

"You know I love you David, but that's pushing it," the Sheriff teased.

Lowe gave her his best sad look, the type that only someone in love can give.

"Alright stop giving me those Meathead eyes. If you're still at it when I get off, I'll come help. Now eat your eggs," she said giving in to his look.

Lowe helped the Sheriff feed her horses after breakfast was over. It seemed like the least he could do after she cooked his breakfast. It was only part of the reason behind his help. He found it hard after their night of love to tear himself away from her; that and he was in no hurry to dive into the boxes of records that awaited him.

It wasn't hard for Lowe to find the documents he had the warrant for. Seven large boxes of computer-generated printouts were stacked on his bed. He had two questions before him: did the boxes contain the pieces to the puzzle and would he find them before retirement.

"Well Meathead, where should we start?" he asked the pup that was probably thinking, "Cool dad, look at all the paper I have to shred."

Lowe decided he would go over Mrs. Brown's phone logs first, mainly because it was the smaller of the boxes. His thoughts were to start small then work his way up; that way his task would not overwhelm him.

He had a pretty good idea what he was looking for because he had a new theory. He hadn't shared it with anyone because his record with ideas of the case hadn't panned out too well. This idea had to be it; he was all out of reasons of anything else it could be.

The box containing the phone logs might have been small but it still took until early afternoon to get through them all. He found one number that peaked his interest, a number that had been called with considerable frequency. It was a number that did not belong to Mr. Brown, Kelly Sue Brown or any other people she might have called with such repetition.

Lowe really didn't feel the need to call Austin to have the techs find out who the number belonged to. It might take a day or two for them to get back to him. The most logical thing was to dial the number himself and see who answered.

Lowe retrieved his cellphone from its charger and entered the digits.

"Good afternoon, Dr. Southerland's office," came a woman's greeting on the other end of the line.

"Sorry, I dialed the wrong number," was Lowe's excuse.

It was plausible that there was a sick horse on the ranch; it might explain the number of calls. The pattern is what stuck out the most: an average of five calls a day, going back three months. The heaviest calling was the four weeks prior to the time the stud had been killed.

It was a red flag but by itself, it wasn't enough evidence to hang his hat on. He needed more and hoped to find more in the remaining boxes. Lowe pushed on through the mountain of documents.

It was a little past three in the afternoon when Kelly came calling. Lowe's eyes were beginning to hurt by then. He jumped at the chance to walk across the street for a cup of coffee with his friend.

"I ain't heard from you since the other night," said Kelly after they were seated. "I thought I best come check on you."

"I'm sorry, me and Marcia made a quick trip to South Texas. We got in late last night. I was going to call you but you saw what awaited me in my room," Lowe explained.

"I'll bet that was romantic. I am surprised you had the time with everything happening around here," Kelly remarked in not so subtle a way.

No Shawn, we went there working on the case. Who pissed in your oatmeal?" Lowe asked, questioning his friend's attitude.

"I'm sorry David, I just have a lot on my mind. It's like I don't know what's gonna happen next and the uncertainty is wearing on me like the wrong bit. Now that Brown is dead, who knows what direction that crazy bitch he was married to is headed," Kelly confessed.

"You know you can always go back to Jonah's, he left it to both of us," Lowe pointed out.

"I know, but that ain't it, Kelly said with a look of concern. It's Kelly Sue I'm worried about. What is going to happen to her. She lives for those horses. It's all she's ever had. Brown was never there but he made sure that his money was. I know it sounds like a small consolation, but that's all she knows."

"It's going to be fine. Who would have ever guessed you'd be the one who was the worrywart," Lowe said trying to console his friend.

"You're probably right." Kelly did his best to agree.

"Speaking of Brown, when is the service?" Lowe asked partly out of respect and partly because of the cop in him.

"Next Tuesday, I have to pick up Kelly Sue Monday," was Kelly's answer.

"Who knows, something might pop by then," Lowe said.

"You have anything?" Kelly's ears perked up at the statement.

"I've got an idea I am playing with," Lowe let it be known.

"You care to share," was his friend's response.

Lowe was reluctant to tell anyone about his latest theory of the case but his friend was in need of a little hope.

"This is just an idea. I have nothing to support it with you must understand. What if Mrs. Brown wanted out of the marriage but wanted to keep her style of life. Brown's attorney told me there was a prenuptial agreement.

"The only thing of any value she could take from the marriage was Double Ds Delight and he was fixing to be worthless. So she cooks up the scheme to kill the horse for the insurance, then I show up and throw a monkey wrench into her plan.

"She's already killed the horse and shit was going hit the fan when Brown figured out what she was up to. It didn't end too well for the last wife, so she decides to go for the whole ball of wax and has Brown taken out.

"It's a good theory, but that's all I have right now and we both know my theories ain't panned out too well as of late," Lowe said after relating his latest idea to his friend.

"I don't like it but it makes sense," was about all Kelly had to say.

"It might make sense, but until I find out who her accomplice was and can prove it, it's just a idea and I have had a bunch of them. Speaking of which I best be getting back before Meathead eats something or craps on something," Lowe joked as he laid a dollar tip on the table.

Lowe was halfway through his paper maze by seven o'clock when he saw car lights shining off the wall. He looked out the window and saw the Sheriff unloading some bags from her back seat. Lowe rushed to the door to help her.

"I brought supper," she said before entering. "My Lord, what happened in here? David, it looks like a paper bomb went off. I am surprised you haven't lost little Meathead in this mess," she said after entering the room.

"I've been so busy, I haven't really noticed," he told her as he looked around the place.

"I brought some takeout, you probably haven't eaten have you?" the Sheriff surmised.

"Nope! I did have a cup of coffee with Shawn a few hours ago," came Lowe's answer.

"Why don't you clear those papers off the table and I'll go get our drinks out of the car," Selter suggested.

He did as he was told when she disappeared out the door. He was beginning to understand why he had fallen in love with her; how could he not?

"What is an all-nighter without takeout and beer?" she asked, returning with a six-pack.

"Sheriff Selter, you are my kind of cop," Lowe said smiling ear-to-ear, right before kissing her.

He told her about the visit he had with Kelly and how upset he seemed to be. She listened and nodded here and there.

"Have you found anything in the boxes yet," the Sheriff asked, after they had finished eaten.

"Maybe! I don't know. I have an idea but I can't seem to find much to support it," Lowe said before explaining the theory he had earlier told Kelly.

"I tell you what, you go take Meathead for a long walk. You need some fresh air and maybe it will clear your head. I'll start in on the remaining boxes while you are gone," she said.

It was midnight, the beer was gone and they had started drinking coffee. Lowe was at the point where he was about to throw in the towel.

"David, David I think I found something," Selter exclaimed.

"What Jimmy Hoffa," said the worn-out man trying to joke.

"Come look at this. I've been going through these credit card records. I've found that at least twice a month there is a charge from the Biltmore Hotel in Oklahoma City. I have compared them with John Brown's credit card statements and found he was nowhere near there," said the Sheriff, reporting her findings.

"Can you tell when the pattern began?" Lowe asked moving closer to her.

"About three months ago. What do you thank it means?" she asked.

"It means I am going to Oklahoma City in the morning. It also means this day is over and not a minute too soon," he declared, throwing a handful of papers in the air.

"Now for the most important question left to answer," she said looking directly at him.

"Please, please, no more questions. I don't think I can handle any more tonight," Lowe cried out falling back on the bed.

"You're going to like this one, I promise," she said in a soft but playful voice.

"Alright, hit me with your best shot," he said giving in.

"Your place or mine?" came the question.

Lowe took one look around the room before answering. "Yours!" he said, delivering his one-word response.

Lowe was back at it by nine the next morning. His first order of business was to call the motel in question and talk with the manager. He had questions he wanted to ask before making the two-and-a-half-hour drive.

Mrs. Brown could have many reasons for her frequent trips to Oklahoma City. She might have a sick relative or friend for example. If that were the case, their smoking gun would have misfired.

"Yes sir Officer Lowe, I know Mrs. Brown. She and Mr. Brown stay with us quite often," the manager stated.

It was about all he needed to hear. He knew then they were onto something. He told the man he'd be there before noon.

"I think we have something, Marcia," he said before grabbing his coat and kissing her goodbye.

Lowe had a sense of elation as he turned on to I-35. He was closer than he had been in a month to finding some answers and perhaps even solving his case. His thoughts turned to the future, something he hadn't allowed himself to do since taking on the assignment.

It was a nice feeling knowing there could be something more than the job. He had no inclination what that might be but he was looking forward to discovering it. He knew whatever it was, that he wanted Selter to be a part of it.

The two-and-a-half-hour drive flew by like nothing. Lowe was pulling into the parking lot before he knew it.

"I'm here to see Mr. Salazar," he told the lady at the front desk.

"You must be Officer Lowe. He has been expecting you. His office is down the hall, third door on your left," the lady told him.

"Officer Lowe, this morning when you called I had just walked in the door. I've since then looked over the records. Believe it or not, the Browns stayed with us last night," the motel manager informed him after they had introduced themselves.

"Mr. And Mrs. Brown stayed here last night? That is very hard to believe," Lowe committed.

"No it's right here in the records, see," the manager said while turning his computer screen around to face Lowe.

"Mr. Salazar, John Brown couldn't have stayed here last night; he's been dead for three days. I doubt if the real John Brown ever stayed here. I would like to know what the man looked like that did stay here," Lowe told the man.

The manager was taken aback at first to hear of Brown's death. He then almost became defensive, telling Lowe it was his job to make sure everyone was who the said they were. It wasn't his place to prevent people from cheating on their spouses.

"Sir, do I look like the sex police?" Lowe asked. "I'm here to conduct a murder investigation. I am not accusing you of anything, I'm just asking questions," he continued, setting the manager straight

"I am sorry Officer Lowe, it's just that people sometimes think it's my job to enforce morality," the manager said as he apologized.

"Can you tell me what your Mr. Brown looks like?" was Lowe's next question.

"I would say he was about your age, nearly six-feet tall with brown hair," the man said trying to be as descriptive as possible.

The man might have tried his best, but there was a name for the person he described: average. Lowe knew if that was all he had to go on, he was gonna need a bigger jail.

"Can you tell me what time they checked out?" was Lowe's second question.

"Just one minute," the man said as he picked up his phone.

Salazar's call was to the front desk in the lobby. The woman Lowe had spoken with earlier said that

Mrs. Brown had left right after the complimentary breakfast. She did not see the man playing the role of Mr. Brown with her. Salazar conveyed the information to Lowe after hanging up the phone.

"Is there a chance the man is still here?" seemed to be Lowe's next logical question.

"I don't think that corridor of rooms have been cleaned yet, so yes," was the manager's answer.

Lowe asked if security could meet him at the room after obtaining its number.

Salazar was on the phone making the request as Lowe was leaving his office.

"Hotel security," the guard repeated twice after knocking.

Lowe and the security guard didn't hear any response from the other side of the door. The guard then opened the door to the empty room.

"I could get lucky," Lowe muttered to himself.

Lowe's next move was to call the Oklahoma City Police Department. He requested that lab techs come to process the room and waited until they arrived on the scene. He left for Whitesboro shortly after they began their work.

Lowe tried to call Sheriff Selter to report his findings but could get through to her office. He tried again thirty minutes later, only to find out that there had been a bad car accident on Highway 377. The Sheriff was on the scene and would be for the foreseeable future, or so said Gracy.

Lowe thought about what he had in relation to the case: conjecture, theory and proof of infidelity. It wasn't near enough to hang a murder charge on the pretty neck of JJ Brown.

He thought about dragging her ass in the next morning for questioning but he knew she would come armed with Lawyer Thigpin. His case of murder was just as flimsy as his fraud case had been. Lowe had no doubt the ending would have been the same.

He then had an idea to go to The Double D Ranch to see her as soon as he returned. Perhaps if he confronted her with what he knew and did a little bluffing, the woman might buckle. A quick confession would put the case to rest once and for all.

It was nearly dusk when Lowe turned off of Highway 82 onto the smaller road that led to the Double D Ranch. He noticed a slight chill in the air; it was a front that had been forecast.

Lowe saw the lights in the main house as he pulled through the gate. JJ Brown's BMW was parked in the driveway. Lowe took it as a good sign that she was home, and hopefully alone. He parked his vehicle next to hers and got out. The hood of his suspect's car was warm to the touch; it hadn't been there much more than an hour.

A long, twisting sidewalk led to the front door on the south side of the dwelling. Lowe saw the door was open when he made the last turn of the sidewalk.

"Mrs. Brown, it's Officer Lowe," he called out after ringing the doorbell. His call was met with silence. He repeated his call and he rang the bell once more, and again it was met with silence.

He thought about walking down to the stables but there was something about the moment that didn't seem right. He reached for his service revolver and ventured inside the Brown estate.

"Mrs. Brown it's officer Lowe; are you alright?" Lowe repeated, walking through the kitchen and then into the living room.

He saw there was a light on in one of the rooms down the hall. Slowly he moved with his gun drawn, making his way to the light.

Bookshelves lined the walls and an oak desk sat in the center. The room appeared to be a study.

At first glance, he saw nothing out of the normal. Lowe was about to turn to leave when he saw two bare legs on the floor protruding from one side of the desk.

"This can't be good," he said to himself.

Behind the massive oak desk, he found a female body lying face down in a pool of blood. Lowe gently rolled the body over to check for any signs of life, as well as to identify who it was.

Just as he thought, the face belonged to JJ Brown. He placed two fingers on her neck to feel for a pulse. There was none, even though the body was still warm. Lowe followed the stream of drying blood to a small bullet hole in the woman's stomach. He looked around the room for a weapon and found none in sight.

"Damn, this is turning into a Shakespearean nightmare," he grumbled, knowing he was back on the who-done-it merry-go-round.

He was in the process of making a call to report what he had found to the Sheriff's office and the DPS office when he heard his name being called from down the hall.

"David, are you in here?" Lowe recognized the voice.

"In here Shawn, don't touched anything," he advised.

"Don't touch anything. My God, is she ...?" Kelly's voice drifted off when he was close enough to see the body.

"Dead, yes, but she hasn't been for long. I want you to back your way out of here and wait for me outside," Lowe instructed his old friend.

Lowe made the calls he intending to make before Kelly's arrival on the scene. The Sheriff still had her hands full with the wreck on Highway 377. Evidently on oil transport truck had hit a van full of senior citizens. The update he received from the dispatcher was that the truck had burst into flames and four of the elderly were known to be dead.

She told Lowe she would have to call a few off-duty deputies and get them out there. His next call was to the DPS where he didn't fair much better. They too were on the scene of the crash.

It was suggested to him to call the Sherman office; perhaps they could send some units out. Lowe had no choice but to follow their advice. The sergeant on duty agreed to dispatch two cars to Lowe's location. He told Lowe their ETA (estimated time of arrival) was thirty minutes.

Lowe knew there was little he could do before the cavalry showed up so he went to find Kelly. He knew Kelly must have been feeding the horses when the woman was killed, he might have heard or seen something.

He was about to ask him when his phone rang. "Officer Lowe," he said when answering it.

"If you're still looking for Garret Mise, you might try the McNutt place out on Country Road 126," the muffled voice said.

"Who is this? Hello, hello," Lowe asked but the caller had already hung up.

"Do you know where the old McNutt place is?" Lowe asked Kelly.

"I need you to stay here and wait for the officers. Tell them I had to go. I then need you to get hold of Marcia and tell her to meet me out there ASAP," he told Kelly after the man had given him directions to the old McNutt place.

"Watch your ass," Kelly warned. "They say that old place is haunted."

Lowe tried to put the pieces of the puzzle together as he drove but they just wouldn't fit. JJ Brown's lifeless body and the anonymous caller blew the case wide open and Lowe's theory right out of the water.

The name Garret Mise kept popping up; the evidence in the stud's death led to Mise. The vehicle that killed Brown belonged to the boy and the faceless caller's unknown voice. What was it about Mise? Could he really be the one behind all of it? Lowe was asking himself those questions as he sped through the night.

Lowe drove through the rickety old gate Kelly had told him about. He turned his lights off halfway down the narrow lane. Up on a hill, he saw a faint light coming from an ancient farmhouse.

Two hundred yards from the place, he brought his car to a stop. Lowe checked his weapon and prepared to go in on foot. The easiest path was straight down the road, but he chose going around through the underbrush to avoid being ambushed.

The closer he got to the house, the faster his heart began to beat. All his senses became attuned to his surrounding as he circled around behind the house. He thought it might be best to come in through the back door so he could get the drop on whoever was inside.

The boards on the back porch began to creak under his feet, but there was little he could do about it. Lowe prayed the sound of a brisk wind would mask the sharp pitch of the creaking.

Lowe reached out for the nineteenth-century doorknob, and turned it. The door opened immediately with little effort. The ease in which it opened told him it had been used recently.

The first room was dark but he could see light ahead of him radiating from the front of the house.

Slowly he moved, one step after the other. One last step and he would be upon whatever awaited him.

Lowe burst into the room with his gun drawn. "State Trooper," he loudly announced.

The room was bare, all but for an old sofa in a dark corner. He could see a figure sitting there lifeless. He shined his flash on the person.

"Alright let me see your hands," Lowe demanded before it registered that the person was already dead and had been for sometime.

Lowe could tell through the frost on the thawing body that it was Garret Mise. He was about to take a step forward when he heard a click behind him. Lowe didn't have to guess what made the sound; he knew it was a hammer being cocked on a gun.

"All right Lowe, drop the pistol and turn around," a voice ordered from behind him.

Lowe didn't have to wait to face the man to know who he was,. He had heard the voice before and knew it belonged to Dr. Jason Southerland.

"You don't look too surprised, Lowe," Southerland said coming into the light.

"I'm not, I always knew you had some kind of hand in this. I just never figured you as the mastermind," Lowe committed.

"Mastermind you say, of what? It has been nothing but one mistake after another. No one was supposed to die - just kill the horse, collect the money and run off with JJ.

I was just fixing to put Double Ds Delight down when that kid came in. I guess he knew what I was up to and tried to stop me. As you can see, it didn't end too well for him. I didn't mean to kill him but I panicked. He went for the door and I hit him in the head with a shovel," Southerland explained.

"I guess when I started poking around, the boy came in handy as a patsy," Lowe said, stating the obvious. "I mean it wasn't like he could say otherwise."

"Yes, it all went to hell in a hand basket when you showed up. It was like deja vu all over again. It was not the first time your meddling screwed up my plans," Southerland confessed.

"How do you figure?" Lowe asked with a confused look.

"I had a sweet deal going with Brown and Sanchez on the border before you and that Texas Ranger stumbled onto it. It was my idea to implant dope in those worthless old nags and run them across the border.

I made a shitload of money before the deal went belly up. Damn fool I am, I blew every dime of it. Sanchez and Brown wrote me off after they had no more use for my expertise. I was forced to go back to my boring vet practice and I was pissed," Southerland recounted.

"You're the one that notified the Feds as a way to get even," said Lowe as he was figuring it out.

"You're damn right!" said Southerland. "I wanted to get even but calling the FBI wasn't my smartest move. I was drunk off my ass at the time. It occurred to me when I sobered up that if they caught wind of it, I was a dead man. It would be nothing for Sanchez to send one of his goons after me.

"It's the same reason why I had to kill Brown. When you told me you were on your way to see him, I knew it was only a matter of time before he figured out that me and JJ were having an affair. The money she would inherit, made it make more sense because I figured out the payout on the horse was no longer a sure thing," came the man's reasoning.

Now what? What's your plan now? You kill a cop and they'll give you the needle," Lowe pointed out.

"You don't leave me much of a choice," deduced Southerland. "I knew you were closing in. You didn't see me at the motel today but I saw you. Besides, I'm not going to kill a cop, he is," Southerland said pointing to the lifeless body. "You came looking for Mise, the boy shot you and right before you died, you shot him."

"You don't think they are smart enough to figure that boy's been frozen for a month?" Lowe asked him.

"It won't matter. By then I'll be on the beach in some country that doesn't have a extradition treaty with the U.S.," Southerland said with a laugh as he aimed to shoot Lowe.

"Answer one question before you pull the trigger," directed Lowe, killing time before he met his fate. "Why did you kill Mrs. Brown? That was like killing the goose that laid the golden egg. Were you afraid she might turn on you if she got squeezed hard enough?"

A confused look appeared on the man's face. "JJ is dead?" he said.

The man would never ask another question. A shot rang out as a window shattered. Southerland crumpled to the floor, blood pouring from his chest. In a fraction of a second, Lowe's case was over.

"David, are you alright in there?" a man's voice called from the darkness.

"I'm alright Shawn. Is Marcia with you?" Lowe called back.

"No, I couldn't reach her," Kelly answered.

"Good, 'cause I think I shit my britches," Lowe exclaimed.

The young boy's body was the first thing Kelly saw when he walked in. "Poor kid, he'll never have a future," the horse trainer said as tears formed.

"If you hadn't showed up when you did old buddy, I wouldn't have had one either. I thought I was a goner," Lowe confessed.

The small hamlet of Whitesboro had just come through an extremely eventful day - a day like no other in recent memory. The population of the county had declined by seven, in a twenty-four-hour period.

Five souls were lost in the tragic vehicle accident on the highway, Mrs. JJ Brown had been murdered and the county was minus one veterinarian. Some wondered if there was enough space in the local newspaper for all the headlines that would surely hit the following morning.

Sheriff Selter arrived at the old McNutt place thirty minutes before the mop-up was complete. She found Lowe talking with one of her deputies on the scene. The two didn't have to ask the other how their day had gone; it was written on their faces.

"Just the woman I needed to see," Lowe said the moment he saw her.

"Right back at you, Officer Lowe," she responded with a smile.

"Let me have a word with Shawn, then we can call it a day," he told her.

"What is Shawn doing here?" she asked with surprise in her voice.

"It's a long story, but the short of it is, if not for Shawn, I wouldn't be here. I know it's confusing, but I'm just too tired to explain it," was his answer.

It was going on two in the morning by the time Lowe's head hit the pillow. His thought was that the end of a day had passed its expiration date hours earlier. It was a long sleep he wanted; his reward for a job well done.

Falling to sleep wasn't as easy as he thought it was going to be. Lowe tossed and turned; ten minutes on his left side, ten on his right, then forty five minutes looking up at the ceiling. His mind just wouldn't seem to turn off.

He was back at the abandoned farmhouse, replaying the events. Something wasn't adding up. Lowe first thought it was his close brush with death that kept him from sleeping. He soon figured it wasn't that at all.

It was the last words Southerland had spoke, "JJ is dead?" that were haunting him. He hadn't thought about them until he was trying to sleep. What did the man mean? Was he saying he didn't kill her and he didn't know who did?

Lowe couldn't take it any longer and got up.

"Where are you going?" Selters asked half asleep.

"I can't sleep. I'll go in the front room. I don't want to keep you from yours," he answered, and she was too tired to talk him out of it.

He went over it time after time, reliving every second of the past day. He just couldn't put his finger on it so he paced back and forth. Lowe went to the kitchen to get a drink of water and saw the report of Jane Brown's suicide still lying on the bar. He picked it up and went back to the living room with it.

Lowe pored over the handwritten documents, driven by a need for finding answers. He didn't know why he focused on the suicide report but something in his gut told him the answer had to be there. He read each page twice and when they yielded nothing he turned to the photographs.

He was beginning to think he was wrong; there were no answers to be had in the report. He was about to give up when he saw something in one of the photos he hadn't noticed before.

A small cedar box sat on the coffee table above Jane Brown's body. He had seen the box before but not in the Brown home. He suddenly realized that he had seen the cedar box in Kelly's office at the barn.

Lowe couldn't believe what he was considering but he knew the pieces fit. The only question was "why."

It was six-thirty in the morning when Lowe pulled in the front gate of the Double D Ranch for the last time. He drove past the main house that was still adorned with the yellow crime scene tape and past the barn, where he had first stopped the day the stud was killed. He didn't stop until he was at Kelly's barn.

Lowe didn't see the horse trainer's truck anywhere but it was still early.

He decided to wait for his friend in his office; he might even have a look in the cedar box.

Neither the barn nor the office was locked; Lowe didn't think it would be. Kelly was the type of person who never locked anything. He figured if someone wanted it bad enough, they would take it anyway.

Lowe took the small box in his hand and opened it. The contents of the box revealed the side of Kelly he had never seen before: a man in love. There were letters written years before from Jane Brown to Kelly.

Lowe got half way through one when he heard his friend drive up. He put the letters back and waited for what would surely be the hardest conversation in his life.

Kelly knew something was wrong the minute he walked in. The look on Lowe's face said it all.

"I guess you figured it out. I was going to tell you anyway," Kelly said slumping down in his chair behind his desk.

"Why, in God's name why?" Lowe asked, his heart breaking.

"I'll tell you why, but I have to tell you a few other things first. You might as well keep your seat; it's gonna be a long talk," Kelly told his oldest friend.

"I got all day, Shawn," was Lowe's response.

"Do you remember how we used to ask why Jonah never run me off after all the trouble me and you got into? Old Jonah asked me if I knew the answer right before he died. I told him I didn't have a clue; he wasn't the type for giving second chances.

I'll never forget his answer, not as long as I live. He said I was too much like my daddy," said Kelly as his eyes began to fill with tears.

"I didn't think you knew who your daddy was," a confused Lowe said.

"I didn't, and I damn sure didn't think Jonah knew either. I thought it was the drugs talking at first but he was quick to scold me for thinking such. He then told me about a letter he had received from my mother before she died.

My mother and your daddy were dating before he met your mother. I guess they broke up before she knew she was carrying me. She had seen your folks together and knew they we happy so she never said a word; not to me, your daddy, no one. I reckon her last wish was for me to have a family. That's why she wrote Jonah," Kelly told his half brother about the secret he had carried for years.

"Why in the hell didn't you ever say anything?" Lowe demanded to know.

"Hell David, your daddy was like a God to you. You kept him on a pedestal. Who was I to knock him off of it," Kelly answered.

"Why in the hell are you telling me now?" was Lowe's next question.

"I guess it's because the apple doesn't fall too far from the tree. You see Kelly Sue is my daughter. I fell in love with her mother a year before Kelly Sue was born.

"You see this old, cedar box? I bought it for her in Jackson, Mississippi at the Dixie Nationals. She told me later on that night that Kelly Sue was my child.

"We planned to run away together when we got home. I guess Brown came home and found her packing and killed her. I don't think she ever told him about me or the baby. It's probably why he didn't kill me too. I ran up to the house when I heard the gun shot. I found her lying in a pool of blood. Part of me died with her that day. I went back after all the cops had left and grabbed the box and it's been sitting there ever since," Kelly said, weeping as he told his story.

"Some detective I am. With a name like Kelly Sue, you would think I would have figured that part out. Why didn't you ever say anything?" Lowe asked.

"Why! Well as bad as I hated Brown, I knew he could give Kelly Sue the things I couldn't. I'm kind of like my mother in that respect. As long as I was able to watch her grow up, it was enough," Kelly explained.

"Alright now that we've established who everybody's father is, tell me about last night," Lowe said, bringing the conversation back to the reason why he was there.

"I thought all day what you had told me the day before. How JJ had killed Brown for the money," said Kelly. "I guess I had an idea before you ever said anything. What comes around goes around. I guess John Brown found out karma was a bitch.

"It started me thinking: if you couldn't prove it, what would stop her from killing Kelly Sue for the rest of the money at a later date?

"I went up to the house to confront her and by then she had too much wine to drink. We fought about Brown's murder and she said I'd never prove she had anything to do with his murder; no one would.

"She fired me and asked me to leave but I didn't. She pulled a pistol from the desk door. David, it was the same gun that Brown had killed my Jane with. I guess I saw red. I rushed her, we fought over the gun and it went off. I got scared and got the hell out of there.

I was fixing to get in my truck when I saw you drive up. I actually, believe it or not, went up there to tell you what happened. I was about to when you got the call from Southerland. You know me David; I wouldn't hurt anyone, yet last night I killed two people," Kelly said as he brought his confession to a close.

Lowe just sat there, like he was in shock. He didn't know what to say. It took awhile to take it all in. During a single conversation, he had solved the case, gained a niece and a brother. And more than likely, he lost a brother – at least for awhile.

"I don't know what to say, I damn sure don't know what to do," Lowe told the man.

"I do, you can get off your ass and do your job. You can make our daddy proud," Kelly said in that familiar voice that was Shawn Kelly.

"But Shawn, you're my brother," Lowe said, with a tear about to fall.

"I didn't tell you that to save my ass. I told you so you would watch out after my daughter. Now get off your ass and put the cuffs on me," the horse trainer said.

"Shit Shawn, just go get in the damn car," was about all that was said.

EPILOGUE

Two years had passed since David Lowe had solved the Brown case. It was to be his last case. Officer Lowe resigned from the force as soon as all the paperwork was completed.

He had fulfilled his dream of following in his father's footsteps. He was off to chase some new dreams, like that crazy old cowboy he had met in Austin that day long ago. Lowe didn't make it as far as the islands like Bubba Lee and his dog, instead he settled for a small veterinarian practice in Whitesboro, Texas.

Shawn Kelly, with the help of his little brother, had received a five-year sentence. He was in charge of a string of horses in the Texas Department of Correction's system.

The Feds had moved in and taken most of the Brown estate. Lowe had gone to the Federal dispersal sale, and with a loan from Defoe, bought Kelly Sue's horses back for her.

It was eight in the morning in a quaint little ranch house on the out skirts of Whitesboro. Lowe sat drinking a cup of coffee and reading the morning paper with Meathead at his feet.

The dog had gone from an ugly pup to a full-grown, ugly dog, but Lowe loved him. Meathead went on all the farm calls with his master. It wasn't long before he was well known throughout the county.

"I didn't know you were back from taking Kelly Sue to school," Lowe's wife, the Sheriff, said.

"I got back a little bit ago, Marcia. I thought I'd enjoy my paper before going to work," he told her.

"Good, here hold your son while I finish getting ready for work," his wife ordered.

"Come here to your daddy, little Wade," Lowe said holding his arms out to receive the toddler.

Little Wade, as he was affectionately called by his parents, had been born the spring before. The youngster was named Wilson Wade Lowe, in memory of Lowe's first Captain who had died in the line of duty on the border.

"Have you read that letter you got yesterday from your brother," she asked coming out of the bathroom.

"Yes, I read it last night. He's doing good and says that with good behavior, he'll be home for the cutting futurity. He wants me to get Junior ready for him," said Lowe, relaying his brother's thoughts.

"That's good; he and Kelly Sue showing together, just like old times," Marcia Lowe remarked coming into the room.

"I'm ready, let me have Little Wade. I have to drop him off at Gracy's and then get to work," she said before kissing her husband goodbye.

"Me and Meathead are gonna be leaving as soon as I finish my paper. I'll see you and Little Wade tonight," he told his wife.

Lowe was about to leave for work when he remembered the television was on. When he went to turn it off, his jaw almost hit the floor. He saw Ranger Lucius Defoe's picture on the screen. He turned the volume up so he could hear what they were saying about his old friend.

"We are standing outside the correction unit where yesterday, a highly decorated Texas Ranger, Lucius Defoe left with a female inmate on death row. No one has seen either one since. The Federal Marshals have now been called in. Ranger Defoe is considered a wanted fugitive," was the breaking news flash.

"My God Lucius, what have you got yourself into now?" Lowe muttered in disbelief.

This book has been brought to you by

J.W. Brook's Hats
Gravette, Arkansas

Double J Ranch
Whitesboro, Texas

Rambling Trails Boots
Cleburne, Texas

Shadle Construction
Springtown, Texas

J & S Saddlery
San Angelo, Texas

Tire Outlet Inc.
Boyd, Texas.

Wild Horse Press
Walnut Springs, Texas

Equine Mercantile
Boyd, Texas

AllAboutCutting.com
Boyd, Texas.

Boyd Built
Boyd, Texas

Capital Hatters
Stephenville, Texas

Kelly Horse Shoeing
Boyd, Texas

Shinolas
Springtown, Texas

A special thanks goes out to Susan, Ty, Tyla, and Brandon Hairrell and all of my readers. Thanks guys.

CPSIA information can be obtained at www.ICGtesting.com
Printed in the USA
LVOW120934270613

340494LV00001B/2/P